HENS RULE

By

Susan Weekley

World Castle Publishing

World Castle Publishing
Pensacola, Florida
Copyright © Susan Weekley 2012
ISBN: 9781938243424
First Edition World Castle Publishing June 15, 2012
http://www.worldcastlepublishing.com

Cover: Karen Fuller
Photos: iStock
Editor: Maxine Bringenberg

Dedication

Dedicated to my children and family for all your loving words of encouragement.

Susan Weekley

Acknowledgements

I would like to thank my sister Dorothy for providing the information I needed about chicken farms. Your stories about farm life are always entertaining.

Special thanks to my co-workers who proofread and supported my decision to write.

To my readers:

Please make note that all characters in this story, although they may resemble a living person, are fictitious. However, the town of Evergreen, Alabama is real and is where I was born. For the sake of this story I have relocated the sheriff's office.

Susan Weekley

HENS RULE

Prologue:

There was no use screaming; no one was around to hear her anyway. Her mind was trying to understand why this man wanted to kill her, and at the same time wondering how to get away from him. The wound to her shoulder was making her whole arm go numb. Holding her right arm with her left, she peeked out from behind the chicken house to see if she could find him. Where could she hide from this mad man? Where was he? Thinking she saw him sneaking into the far end of the long building, she ran to the silo and began climbing the ladder. The pain in her shoulder was starting to get worse and climbing was not easy. She was half way to the top of the silo when she heard him calling her.

"Darlyn, what do you think you're doing? You know you can't get away from me. You think I can't see you up there?"

"Keep away from me!" she screamed.

"Oh, come on Darlyn, you know I'm not going away. You want to know why I'm not? Because I'm gonna kill you is why." Steadily he climbed the ladder behind her, but not too fast; he wanted to play with her for a while before he killed her.

Desperately trying to get away from him, she realized too late that climbing the silo was a dumb idea. Her only option now was to keep climbing. The twenty-three foot silo was full of chicken feed and could suffocate a person if they were to fall into it. *Of course! That's it*! she thought. Still climbing, she knew she had to get to the loading door and open it before he reached her. If she could somehow get the door open and push him inside the shaft, she would be safe. Taking a chance, she looked again to see how close he was to her. If she hurried she might get it open in time to push him inside.

Carefully he climbed higher, thinking he could have her any time he wanted. "Why are you trying so hard to get away from me Darlyn?" he asked, "You know I'm gonna get you. Where do you think you can hide up there?" Reaching the top of the ladder he could see that she was desperately trying to open the loading door. "What's the matter Darlyn, you hungry? Ain't nothing in there but chicken feed." Chuckling to himself he made a rush for her.

She barely swung the loading door open before he rushed her.

For a moment the dark and quiet night was assaulted with her screams and his maniacal laughter.

Then there was silence.

Susan Weekley

CHAPTER ONE

The sun beat down on the small cemetery, giving the illusion of a summer day. Although the sunshine was warm, the wind was still blowing strong on this day in May. Standing on the outskirts of the cemetery a lone woman watched her daughter as the young woman lingered by the graveside. News of the death of Darlyn MacKinstry had come as a shock to her sister and niece. Even more shocking was that Darlyn had left everything to her niece.

A city girl born and raised, the last thing Rachel Collier knew anything about was operating a chicken farm. Standing in the warm sunshine looking at her aunt's grave, she wondered what Darlyn could have been thinking. Rachel was a schoolteacher; she had never wanted to be anything else. What did she know about chickens? On the other hand, maybe this was what she needed in her life right now. Maybe she should give it a try. After all, what did she have to go back to in Mobile? Last year she had become engaged to a very socially prominent lawyer in town. Even though Jason Sims was one of Mobile's most sought after catches, she knew in her heart that she had made the right decision to break the engagement. After a year of social events and upper society galas, Rachel had decided she needed more out of her life. She wanted more than what Jason's money could offer—she just wasn't sure what that something was yet. Her friends and family couldn't understand why she would want to give up a chance to live with financial security, not to mention the fact that Jason was easy to look at.

Turning from the graveside, Rachel walked slowly toward her mother. Sherry Collier was still an attractive woman at the age of forty-three. Standing in the sunshine, her hair picked up golden highlights. At four foot ten she was a good four inches shorter than her daughter. Rachel was often told that she looked like her mother, but she had never seen it herself until now.

Reaching Sherry's side, Rachel linked arms with her. "Let's go, Mama."

"Yes, let's go home," Sherry replied.

"No, Mama, I want to go to Darlyn's house." Mentally correcting herself, she thought, *my house now*.

The sun was setting as they drove along Highway 31, and the ride to MacKinstry Farm was brief and silent. Neither Sherry or Rachel spoke on the way. As Rachel slowly drove down the dirt lane leading to the farmhouse, she took in the beauty of the land around her. Maybe this wouldn't be such a bad idea after all. Small rolling hills and neighboring pastures of green dotted with cattle surrounded her farm. She could understand why Darlyn loved living here. The MacKinstry Farm was located in Owassa, Alabama, about 100 miles northeast of Mobile.

Rachel pulled the car into the circular drive and stopped in front of the farmhouse. Stepping out of the car, the women were suddenly hit by the stench associated with raising chickens.

"How Darlyn could live here I'll never know," said Sherry. "Sure, the house is nice, but this smell is awful."

"She always said it smelled like roses to her," Rachel said, laughing at the memory.

Turning to go into the house, both women were startled when they saw a man step off the front porch and walk toward them. He was a bear of a man, towering over both Sherry and Rachel.

Looking at him Rachel guessed him to be in his early fifties. A fine head of hair just going silver at the temples gave him a dignified appearance.

"How you ladies doing today? Let me introduce myself. I'm your neighbor down the road about two miles or so. My name is Oscar Newcume. Just wanted to stop and pay my respects. Yes sir, Ms. Darlyn was a fine lady. We're gonna miss her."

Not wanting to appear rude, Rachel stepped forward and started to shake Mr. Newcume's hand. "Hello, Mr. Newcume, I'm Rachel Collier and this is my mother, Sherry Collier."

"Now you're just trying to fool an ol' man! This can't be your mother—she looks more like your sister to me!"

Laughing, Sherry stepped up to shake Mr. Newcume's hand. "Why thank you, Mr. Newcume. Now I understand why Darlyn liked it here so much. Tell me, are all the men here so charming?"

Irritated with her mother's obvious flirting, Rachel asked, "What can we do for you, Mr. Newcume?"

"Well, I just came by to pay my respects; that's all, Ms. Rachel. Your aunt was a very popular lady around here, and I'm sure you're gonna be getting a lot of visitors. Just wanted to let you know I'll be glad to help you ladies with anything you need…anything at all."

"That's very kind of you Mr. Newcume; if we need anything we'll let you know. For now I think I need to get Mama inside and settled down. This has been very hard on her. You will excuse us, won't you?" Taking Sherry by the arm Rachel almost dragged her to the front steps.

"Does this mean you ladies will be staying in Owassa for a while?"

Embarrassed by her daughter's sudden loss of manners, Sherry answered before Rachel could speak. "We've made no immediate plans Mr. Newcume, but we will be here long enough to finalize the estate. I'm sure we'll see you again."

"Good, good, I'll be looking forward to it. Well, I must be getting back to my place. You ladies need anything you let Ol' Oscar know, okay?"

Sherry waved goodbye as she stood on the front porch watching Oscar drive away. Voicing her irritation toward her mother, Rachel said, "What were you thinking? Why did you encourage him?"

Sherry's face showed how tired and upset both she and Rachel were, but she was not one to mildly stand by and let her daughter chastise her. "I thought he was very friendly and not bad looking.

If I'm going to be stuck in the country, at least I can have someone close to my age to talk to. What's got into you anyway? Ever since you broke up with Jason you've turned into a prude!"

"Excuse me ladies...."

Jumping, both Rachel and Sherry turned to see who this was. Standing at the side of the house was Ollie Hinton. He had been Darlyn's hired help in the chicken house for several years. It was Ollie who'd found Darlyn's body as he was coming to work in the early hours of the morning. Trying to block that image from her mind Rachel focused on what Ollie was saying. "I'm sorry to disturb you. I was needing to know if you still wanted me to come in tomorrow morning."

"Of course we do Ollie. Without you there is no one to run the farm. I'm depending on you to show me the ropes."

"So, you mean you're gonna stay, like you told Mr. Newcume?"

Not wanting to draw attention to the fact that Ollie had been eavesdropping Rachel replied, "Yes. Oh, by the way, how early do you get here?"

"About 4'clock; we always start early. Ms. Darlyn said, 'The hens rule and we have to be ready when they are'." Laughing at the memory, he shook his head and smiled. "That Ms. Darlyn sure was a funny lady. But I expect you know that, huh."

Still obviously frustrated with Rachel, Sherry interrupted, saying, "We'll both see you in the morning Ollie." Her tone of voice and facial expression was one she used when she was displeased with someone.

Seeing the look on Ms. Sherry's face, Ollie stopped smiling. "Okay, see you in the morning. Bye."

Ashamed of the way Sherry was speaking to Ollie, Rachel smiled her sweetest and said bye. Ollie had been a friend of the family long before he came to work for Darlyn and Rachel couldn't let him leave with hurt feelings.

Opening the front door, Rachel paused to look at her new home. The old farmhouse had been remodeled many times over the last fifty years. Every time Rachel came to visit Darlyn she never knew what she would find. Originally the overseers' house for a large plantation, the old house sat on the top of a hill surrounded by pecan and crepe myrtle trees. With each new owner the house was added onto, making it a hodge-podge of architecture with old country charm. A wrap-around porch graced the lower floor. Bay front windows were to the right of the front door where Darlyn's office was located.

The foyer had been stripped down to the old hardwood floors and polished to a beautiful shine. To the left of the foyer was a large parlor. With floor length windows and a twelve-foot ceiling, the room was bright and sunny. Darlyn had redecorated again, but this time Rachel liked what she saw. A comfortable looking couch and love seat faced each other on an old braided rug. A coffee table made of oak sat between the two, making the room very inviting. Antiques were everywhere. Between the two front windows was a roll top desk and chair. The original stone fireplace was on the far wall facing the seating arrangement. Family pictures were proudly arranged on the mantle. In the back far corner was an old Baldwin piano. It had been Darlyn and Sherry's when they were little girls. Darlyn played like an angel, but Sherry, even after years of lessons, still could not read a note. Remembering the fun they had last Christmas in this very room with Darlyn playing Christmas carols and Sherry singing was too much for Rachel. Tears stung her eyes; she still couldn't believe Darlyn was gone.

Seeing the tears forming in Rachel's eyes Sherry went to her and embraced her. "Why don't you go on up and get settled in? I'll lock up down here. We're going to need to try to sleep if we're getting up at 4 A.M."

Knowing that her mother had never gotten out of bed before eight in her life, Rachel looked at her with surprise.

"Don't look at me like that young lady; I can get up with the chickens if I have to!"

With a 'we'll see' expression, Rachel kissed her mother good night and headed up the staircase.

* * * * *

Standing at the counter in the cozy old kitchen, Rachel poured herself a cup of coffee. She could not remember the last time she was up at three o'clock in the morning. Turning to look out the window above the sink, she wondered if she should go wake her mother. Mr. Newcume had been right when he said they would be getting a lot of visitors. Rachel had barely made it to the top of the stairs last night when there was a knock at the front door. Friends of Darlyn's had poured into the house carrying platters and trays of food. Rachel and Sherry greeted each guest with as much enthusiasm as they could given the circumstances. Finally, around eleven o'clock, Roxanne Hinton ushered the last of the guests out the door. Roxanne was Ollie's older sister and had been Darlyn's best friend for over forty years. They had been inseparable since the first grade. After helping to clean up and put away the leftover food, Roxanne left them, saying she would see them tomorrow.

Yawning, Rachel wondered again if she should wake Sherry. At that moment, Sherry stumbled into the kitchen. Blurry eyed, she nudged Rachel out of the way so she could reach a coffee cup. Too short to reach the cups on the second shelf, Sherry looked at Rachel with a silent plea for assistance. This was a routine they had followed since Rachel was thirteen. Secretly Sherry was pleased that Rachel was taller than she was. She had always hated being short and petite. Sherry was a very independent woman and did not like feeling inadequate in any way. Rachel had realized that fact about her mother many years ago, but still could not help herself from teasing Sherry when they were alone. "I'll get it, Shorty," she would say. This time Rachel let it go without making any comment. She just nudged Sherry back, got a cup down and filled it with coffee. Finishing her coffee first, Rachel sighed and said she would meet Sherry at the chicken coops.

The early morning hours cast long and dark shadows around her. As she made her way down the lane behind the farmhouse to the main chicken coop Rachel was glad she had remembered to bring one of the flashlights she'd found on the back porch. It had been many years since she had last made this trip. When Rachel was in high school she would spend her summers helping Aunt Darlyn and

Uncle Mack work the chicken farm. Thinking back to those happier times brought Rachel to tears once again. Darlyn and Mack had been high school sweethearts. Marrying right after graduation, they had settled into the farmhouse with Grandpa Joe. Shortly after that Grandpa Joe died, leaving the farmhouse to Darlyn. Sherry was living in Mobile with Grandmother Barbara. Rachel had never known Grandpa Joe but she had heard all about him from her mother, Aunt Darlyn, and of course Grandmother Barbara over the years.

Hearing a noise to her left Rachel came back to the present. Shining her light to see what the noise was, she came face to face with a kitten caught in some briars on the side of the lane. Wiping the tears off that had been streaming down her face, Rachel bent down to help the little gray fur ball. Frightened and meowing at the top of its lungs, the kitten struggled harder to escape the briars. Rachel spoke softly to the kitten as she untangled it. "Don't be scared, little kitty, I'll help." Finally pulling it free from the last of the thorns, Rachel hugged the kitten to her chest and continued whispering to it. "Why, we're both just being weepy wusses this morning, aren't we?" Taking the kitten with her she started down the lane to the chicken houses.

The magnitude of her inheritance started settling on Rachel's mind and she mentally went over everything she could remember about the farm. MacKinstry Farm was not a chicken farm in the sense that chickens were raised to be sold to market. Oh, they made it there eventually; however, the real purpose of the chicken coops was egg harvesting. Ten years ago Darlyn and Mack had built four additional houses, making a total of six. Each house was 400 feet long and held 8,000 hens and 800 roosters at a time. Three silos sat between the houses. They contained enough feed to supply two houses each. In front of all of them was the main house, where the eggs were cleaned and refrigerated. Stepping inside, Rachel was overcome with a smell of ammonia so strong that it burned her eyes and nose. Still holding the kitten close she looked around. Straight in front of her were the cleaning stations for the eggs that came from the middle two coops. To her right was a bathroom, complete with a walk in shower and a large mop sink. To her left was an old black leather couch that Rachel recognized. It had been Uncle Mack's favorite piece of furniture in the parlor. She suspected Aunt Darlyn couldn't part with it and had put it here to rest on.

A small sleeping child currently occupied the couch. Although Rachel had never seen Ollie's little girl, she knew this must be Molly. Long dark hair spilled over her tanned face. Rachel decided she must favor her mother instead of her daddy, because Ollie was fair skinned with sandy colored hair. Rachel didn't wonder why Molly was here; she had learned from the many letters that Darlyn wrote that Molly's mother, Trina, had run off not long after Molly was born. Ollie said she had gone back to the reservation. Trina was a full-blooded Cherokee Indian, who Ollie had met when he was in the army stationed in Oklahoma. Not wanting to disturb Molly, Rachel placed the kitten at the opposite end of the couch and wrapped it in part of the covers. Snuggling in the old afghan, the kitten curled into a ball and went to sleep. Turning around, Rachel was startled to see Ollie standing there.

At five foot ten inches Ollie was not an intimidating fellow. His serious expressions led people to believe he was older than his twenty-seven years. Because of the age difference between Ollie and Roxanne, Rachel subconsciously thought of him as Roxanne's son instead of her brother. He was a simple man with little to say, always letting other people initiate conversations. This time, however, he spoke first.

"What you got there Ms. Rachel?' he asked while peeking around her.

"I found a kitten in the briars up the lane, and thought I would keep it—you know, as a pet." She had always wanted a pet, but Sherry and Grandmother Barbara would never let her have one.

"Well, okay. I just came out here to check on Molly. She sometimes wakes up and starts wandering around. Ms. Darlyn never minded me bringing her here until time to take her to the church daycare." Nervously he fidgeted with his baseball cap, waiting for her reply.

"It's no problem, Ollie. You ready to get started? I do remember we have to collect the eggs before we start cleaning them."

Looking at Rachel's feet, Ollie told her she might need to swap her tennis shoes for an old pair of rubber galoshes by the bathroom. Darlyn had kept extra pairs in case she had visitors who wanted a tour of the coops. Rachel was swapping her shoes when Sherry waltzed into the chicken house. Mumbling about the early hours, she too swapped her shoes out and followed Rachel into the chicken coop.

Both ladies stood just inside the doorway and got acclimated to their surroundings. The inside of the chicken coop was noisy, smelly and warm. The floor was made of concrete so it could be hosed out during the molting season. Sawdust was spread on the concrete to help absorb the chicken poop. A conveyer belt ran the length of the coop and separated into two sections leading out of a plastic covered flap to the cleaning stations in the main room. Rows of wooden nests were on either side of the conveyer belt. The rows were spaced far enough apart so the chickens could walk around on the floor. This area had to be well ventilated or the ammonia from the chicken poop would be intolerable. Large fans located at intervals down the length of the building pulled the smell out. Chickens were everywhere. Some walked the floor while others flew to the lighting rafters to roost. Following Ollie's lead, they started to work.

After several hours Ollie told the ladies he needed to check on Molly and take her to the daycare. Sweating and smelling like chicken poop, both Rachel and Sherry decided to also take a break. As the trio neared the door to the main room Molly burst in. Her dark brown eyes were shining large and bright with mischief.

Holding the little gray kitten close she yelled, "Look what I found!"

Before Ollie could reach his daughter, the kitten, squirming to escape, jumped out of Molly's grasp and started to run. Rachel and Molly both made a dash for the kitten. Chickens were clucking and running in every direction to get away from the kitten, Molly and Rachel. It was such a funny sight Sherry and Ollie could not contain their laughter. A large white hen flew straight into Rachel's head, causing her to lose her footing. Slipping, she reached out to grab something to break her fall, only to knock Molly down with her. This made Ollie and Sherry laugh that much louder.

Rachel and Molly sat on the floor covered from head to toe in sawdust and chicken poop. Bewildered, Molly looked around, then started to cry. Anger overtook Rachel when she realized her mother and Ollie were laughing at her.

"You think this is funny, huh? Well here!" Taking a large handful of sawdust and poop she flung it at Sherry. With tears of laughter in her eyes, Sherry managed to dodge it.

While Ollie picked up Molly and started toward the door, Sherry gave Rachel a hand off the floor. Turning he spoke to them, "If you don't mind I'll put Molly in the shower here and you can go back to the house to get cleaned up. After she's had her shower I'll take her on to the daycare. It should be open by now."

Scooping the kitten up as it started rubbing her leg, Rachel replied, "Sure, Ollie you go ahead. After I get cleaned up, Mama and I will start cleaning the eggs we collected."

"Okay, Ms. Rachel, I'll be back as soon as I can."

"There's no hurry," Sherry said over her shoulder as she pushed Rachel out the door and into a warm sunny morning.

Susan Weekley

CHAPTER TWO

Sheriff Jake Brewer sat in his Blazer and let the warmth of the sunshine settle in his bones. He had not wanted to make this trip; dealing with bereaved family members was not his idea of fun. Jake had never met Sherry or Rachel Collier and he did not know what to expect. How were they going to react when he told them Darlyn had been murdered? A couple of tearful women were not what Jake wanted to deal with this morning.

With the exception of Mr. Lynch, the county coroner and local mortician, Jake was the only one who knew about the strangulation marks on Darlyn's neck. To protect his investigation he made Mr. Lynch have a closed casket service. He had instructed Mr. Lynch to tell everyone that the fall had messed her face up too badly for him to do a respectable job on. No one had questioned Mr. Lynch, thinking Darlyn had accidentally fallen while checking the silo. But now Jake had some questions that needed answers, and that meant he would have to confide in Darlyn's sister and niece.

As a young man Jake had played football through an academic scholarship at the University of Alabama, but an injury to his knee early in his first season brought an end to his football days. Jake didn't let the injury stop him from getting a bachelor's degree in law and criminology, graduating at the top of his class. After graduation Jake came to Conecuh County as a deputy sheriff for his uncle, Sheriff Russell Brewer. Russell Brewer had been sheriff for over twenty years. Since his retirement six years ago, Jake had been voted into office. Together Jake and Russell had seen many deaths, mostly car accidents out on Interstate 65. They had seen gunshot victims during hunting season, and enough domestic violence to make Jake positive that Darlyn had been murdered.

Not sure if the Collier ladies would be up this early, Jake decided to go straight to the chicken houses first and speak to Ollie. Maybe Ollie had remembered something that might help. The morning Ollie found Darlyn's body he had gone into shock. Taking him back to town to try and get some answers, Jake mistakenly sent Ollie over to see Doc Lowery before he questioned him. The doctor had given Ollie a sedative, which left him unable to answer anything that would help Jake with his investigation.

Pulling the Blazer into the drive in front of the chicken house, Jake could see that Ollie was there; his old Toyota pickup truck was parked under a pecan tree. Stepping out of his vehicle, Jake saw the door of the chicken house open. Expecting it to be Ollie, Jake waited by the Blazer for him.

Stopping suddenly, Rachel was hit from behind by Sherry as they stepped into the bright sunshine.

"Well, go on Rachel; what's wrong?" Standing behind her, Sherry's face showed confusion over what had caused her to stop like that. Peeking around her daughter Sherry could see the source of the situation immediately.

In front of her was an extraordinarily handsome man. He was at least six feet tall and bronzed from the sun, with dark hair and sparkling gray eyes that looked silver in the sunlight. Staring into those eyes one could become mesmerized.

Not sure what to make of the spectacle in front of him Jake suppressed a smile. "Good morning, Mrs. and Ms. Collier, how are you ladies this morning?"

Sidestepping her daughter, Sherry moved protectively in front of Rachel. "We're fine, Sheriff, just had a small mishap, that's all. What can we do for you?"

Obviously embarrassed and angry at being seen with sawdust and chicken droppings covering her Rachel moved away from her mother, saying, "I'm going up to the house to get cleaned up. You can talk to the sheriff, Mama." With that said she took off at a fast walk to the house.

Watching Rachel practically run up the lane, Jake smiled at Sherry and said, "I really need to speak to both of you, Mrs. Collier. Just so you know, I also asked Roxanne Hinton to stop by this morning. This way I can talk to all of you at the same time."

Not sure why the sheriff needed to speak to them, Sherry said, "Okay. Why don't you come up to the house and I'll get you some coffee while Rachel gets cleaned up. And by the way, you can call me Sherry. I don't answer to Mrs. Collier very often."

*　　*　　*　　*　　*

Reaching the back porch Rachel realized she was still carrying the kitten. She hurriedly poured it a saucer of milk in the kitchen and ran up the back stairs to take a shower. Grabbing a bar of lavender and chamomile soap she washed thoroughly, praying the smell would wash away. The sawdust in her hair was another problem. Washing it the best she could and using conditioner, she hoped to get it clean. Stepping out of the shower and inspecting herself briefly in the full-length mirror on the back of the bathroom door, she was satisfied that she had done a thorough job. Dressing in an old pair of jeans and a purple tee shirt, she combed her hair and pulled it into a hair clip, letting it hang down her back.

Coming down the stairs to the kitchen, Rachel could hear voices. She recognized Roxanne's voice, along with her mother's and the sheriff's. Everyone was sipping their coffee as she entered the room and said hello to Roxanne. They were all sitting around the kitchen table, but Rachel went to stand by the sink where she could look into the sheriff's eyes again.

*   *   *   *   *

Jake, who had been speaking to Roxanne and Sherry, stopped in mid-sentence. Standing before him was a stunning blond; about five foot two with dark green eyes framed by long lush lashes. He had never imagined this beautiful creature was under all that sawdust.

Sherry and Roxanne exchanged a quick look of mutual amusement at the tension that exploded between the younger couple. Roxanne spoke, breaking the spell. "You were saying, Jake?"

"Yea...ahh—"

"You were saying you needed to speak to us about Darlyn's death."

Thinking he was acting like a love-starved fool, Jake held out his coffee cup and asked for a refill. While Sherry poured, Jake composed himself and spoke to the ladies with a more professional attitude. "What I'm about to tell you is confidential and I do not want it repeated around town. Mrs. Collier—Sherry, I mean—I know this will be a shock, but I have to tell you that Darlyn did not die accidentally. She was murdered."

"Murdered?" Roxanne gasped, before anyone else could respond. "How? I mean she fell, didn't she?"

"Yes," he replied. Explaining what he knew, he told them about the strangulation marks on Darlyn's neck. Bruises like the ones she had could not have been caused from a fall. Jake noticed that Rachel had moved to the back of Sherry's chair and the two were comforting each other by holding hands. Thinking the women were strong enough to handle the truth, Jake continued. "Both Mr. Lynch and I agree that Darlyn was murdered. That's why I asked him not to let you have an open casket at the funeral."

Rachel reacted to Jake's news without thinking and exploded at him saying, "You mean to tell me we didn't get to properly say good-bye to Aunt Darlyn because you didn't want us to see marks on her neck? Do you know how hard this has been on

Mama?" Appalled and angry, Rachel pulled away from her mother and started to pace the kitchen floor. "Of all the nerve! Who the hell do you think you are? We have a right to know what really happened!"

Jumping to his feet, Jake stepped in front of Rachel. "Now hold on a damn minute, Rachel, I am doing this by the book! I thought it was best under the circumstances. I can't jeopardize my investigation by letting female emotions get in my way!"

Sherry jumped to her feet and took control of the situation, stepping between the two. "Rachel, take the kitten outside and cool off. Now!"

Rachel took one look at her mother's angry face and did as she was told, but not before giving Jake a look that sent daggers into his chest.

Watching to make sure Rachel was okay, Sherry visibly struggled to calm down before she turned to Jake and asked, "So how can we help you, Sheriff?"

Looking at both Roxanne and Sherry he replied, "I need to know if Darlyn ever said anything to either of you about someone threatening her?"

"I haven't spoken to Darlyn in months except by letters," answered Sherry, shaking her head.

Interrupting, Roxanne exclaimed, "Oh my God!" Starting to cry, she put her head in her hands.

Bracing his hands on the edge of the table, Jake softly asked Roxanne what was wrong; had she remembered anything?

"A few weeks ago, Darlyn came into the beauty shop and said she thought a fox had been getting into the chicken houses. She asked to borrow my pistol. You know, the one you helped me get? She said she would rather use it to kill the fox instead of her shotgun. She laughed and said it wouldn't make near as big a mess. Do you think someone threatened her some way, and she really wanted it for protection?"

"I don't know, but I guess it's possible. Did she still have the pistol?"

"Yes; I hadn't seen her since church the Sunday before her accident. I forgot to ask her if she had ever killed the fox."

Straightening, Jake looked at Sherry and asked her if she would look for it in Darlyn's room. Sherry ran up the back stairs to check.

Wiping her eyes, Roxanne spoke to Jake. "I'm sorry I didn't tell you sooner about the pistol, but Jake, I honestly didn't know it was important."

In an effort to comfort her, he said, "You had no way of knowing until now, Roxanne. Thanks for remembering it; it might help."

Slowly descending the stairs Sherry exclaimed, "Here it is! It was in her night stand." Carefully she handed it to Jake. "These things scare me to death; I don't know how you can stand to have it around, Roxanne."

Snapping the chamber open, Jake saw there were only four bullets in it. Looking at Roxanne, he asked, "Was the chamber full when you gave the gun to Darlyn?"

"I think so...yes, I do remember she checked the chamber just like you are doing now before she left the shop. It only had one bullet in it and she asked me where I kept the extras. I told her and then she filled it herself. I remember her saying when she finished, 'That should be enough for the job.' I thought she meant killing the fox."

"Think hard Roxanne, did Darlyn say anything else?"

"No, that's all. If I think of anything else I'll let you know."

"Thanks, ladies, you've been a great help. I'll be in touch." Jake stuck the pistol in the back of his pants, picked up his hat and started for the door.

Leaving Sherry and Roxanne sitting at the kitchen table Jake went outside. He could see

Rachel and the kitten in the gazebo behind the house. Deciding not to make her angry again he kept walking, but he could feel her staring a hole through his back. This made him ignore her even more.

*   *   *   *   *

Rachel watched Jake walk down the lane to the chicken coops where his Blazer was parked. Still angry with him, she thought over what he had told them. Curious about what she had missed Rachel went back to the house. Setting the kitten down in the kitchen, she looked questionably at her mother and asked, "Well, what else did he say?"

Sherry was at the refrigerator pulling out sandwich meat. Sensing that Rachel was still upset, she smiled and said, "Let's go ahead and eat lunch while we're up here, and Roxanne and I will tell you what you missed."

"I'm not hung—"

Using her best imitation of Grandmother Barbara's voice, Sherry interrupted, "You will sit down and make yourself a sandwich, young lady. You didn't eat any breakfast, and it will be a long time before dinner. We still have to clean all those eggs we gathered this morning!"

Even though she was grown, the value of showing respect to her elders was so ingrained in

Rachel's character that she sat down gracefully and asked Sherry to pass the bread.

Hiding a smile behind her hand, Roxanne didn't say a word. She was amused at Rachel's reaction to Sherry's comical imitation of Ms. Barbara.

*   *   *   *   *

Pondering on this new development in his investigation, Jake walked to the chicken house. As he drew near he saw another vehicle parked next to his Blazer. Ollie was standing in front of the cars, talking to a stranger. Seeing Jake coming closer Ollie stopped speaking to the other man and called out to Jake. "Hey Sheriff, I saw your truck; wondered where you were."

Shaking hands with Ollie, Jake replied, "I was up at the main house talking to Mrs. Collier." Turning, he addressed the stranger. "I'm Sheriff Brewer; and who might you be?"

Reaching to shake hands with Jake, the man introduced himself. "Name's Alec Jameson, I'm the feed supplier for the farm. Nice to meet you Sheriff. I heard about what happened to Mrs. MacKinstry when I was in town. Thought I better stop and talk to Ollie here about what's gonna happen to the farm."

"I told Alec he needed to talk to Ms. Rachel, seeing as how it's her farm now."

"Yea, you did. Well, I guess I'll stop by to see her some other time. I have other appointments today and I'm late for one now. You guys have a good day." With that Alec got in his car and left.

Watching him leave, Jake made a mental note to check out Mr. Alec Jameson. "Ollie, what company did he say he was with?" he asked.

Scratching his head Ollie looked at Jake and said, "Don't reckon he did say, but he's alright. Been our feed man for 'bout two years now. Owns Jameson Feed Company over in Andalusia."

Out of the corner of his eye Jake saw the door to the chicken house opening slowly. Peeking out the door was Molly. Catching the direction Jake was looking, Ollie turned around. "You ready, honey?" he asked her. "Come on out here."

Shyly Molly walked out of the chicken house and stood hugging the back of her daddy's leg. "I got to get moving, Sheriff...I have to take Molly over to the daycare. Did you need to see me 'bout something?"

Not wanting to talk to Ollie in front of Molly about Darlyn's death, he said, "Not right now, just came back to get my Blazer. I need to get into town myself." Shaking Ollie's hand again and waving bye to Molly, Jake got in the truck and headed back to town.

*　　*　　*　　*　　*

Watching from behind a boulder on a hill opposite from the chicken house, he could see the sheriff leaving. His boss was right; he had been careless on this job. He had been hiding at the side of the building when the sheriff first drove up. But luck was with him again and he managed to get a safe distance away without being seen. The problem was he couldn't hear what was being said down below. Rising from his hiding place, he winced at the pain in his right lower leg. That damn MacKinstry woman had shot at him last week when he had broken into the farmhouse. The memory of that night still made him angry. Never having been in the house before he wasn't familiar with where everything was, and he had tripped over a small table in the parlor, knocking over a lamp. The noise brought her down the stairs so fast he almost didn't make it out the kitchen door without her seeing his face. But she did fire a couple of shots at him. The first missed by about six inches. The last one caught him in his calf, going straight through.

He went through the woods to the east of the farmhouse and down the hill to where his truck was hidden. Retracing his path, he used an old logging road to get away, following it back to Highway 31 heading for Greenville.

He had always been a drifter, stopping long enough to work a job then moving on. He wouldn't get paid for this one until it was over. The problem was, now he had two more women to deal with. He hated women. They always thought they were better and smarter than him. That's why he didn't mind killing them. He had killed several women over the years and enjoyed making them beg for their stupid lives before he killed them. *God*, he thought, *women are miserable excuses for human beings*.

Stepping on the gas he sped down the twisting road, not even looking at the beautiful scenery around him. He needed to hurry and get to the cabin; the boss would be there about dark and would want a progress report. As he drove, a plan started forming in his mind. He would discuss it with the boss tonight. If everything went as planned he would get his money and be out of this part of the country before long.

* * * * *

The afternoon shadows were lengthening as Ollie drove his pickup from the chicken coop to the farmhouse. Rachel and Sherry were in the cab with him. They had put in a long hard day and he was surprised and proud of their work. Pulling to a stop at the side of the house waiting for them to get out he said, "We did pretty good today. I figure we collected 'bout 7,000 eggs from each house. Not bad for a couple of city slickers like ya'll."

"Is that all we did? It felt more like a 100,000 to me," Sherry replied.

Laughing, Ollie pointed to a dark maroon colored Cadillac parked in front of the house. "Looks like ya'll have company."

Seeing the car, both Sherry and Rachel groaned. They recognized Grandmother Barbara's car and wondered how long she had been waiting. Saying good-bye to Ollie they walked to the front of the house and entered by the front door. They had expected Barbara to be on the front porch but she was nowhere in sight. Not wanting to take any unnecessary chances with their safety, they'd made sure the house was locked when they left after lunch. However, now the front door was unlocked, making them wonder how Barbara had gotten in.

Stepping into the house they could smell food cooking. By the delicious aromas coming from the kitchen, they knew that Grandmother's housekeeper had come with her. When she was younger, Rachel had referred to Dora as the old crow to her friends. She had always been scared of Dora until Sherry told her how Dora used to be a happy person. She would sing along with the radio at the top of her lungs when Barbara wasn't around. When Rachel asked why Dora had turned into a sourpuss, Sherry told her how the man Dora was married to stole all her money and ran off with another woman; she never got over the hurt. After that, Rachel stopped calling her the old crow behind her back.

They found Barbara in the parlor reading a novel and smoking a cigarette. Seeing the pair standing there she looked up, saying, "It's about time you two showed up. Where have you been?" Looking closer at their attire, she wrinkled her nose and said, "Never mind...I can smell you from over here. Go wash that disgusting smell off and get ready for dinner. Dora should have it ready by the time you're through." Waving her hand in the air, she dismissed them.

"Yes ma'am," Rachel replied automatically. "But tell me, Grandmother, how did you get into the house? We made sure it was locked before we left at lunch."

Sitting up to her full height of five-three Barbara retorted, "Have you forgotten this used to be my house long before it was ever yours? Darlyn may have remodeled the inside, but that lock on the front door is ancient. I used my old key." Picking up her novel she again dismissed Rachel and Sherry.

Climbing the front stairs Rachel looked at the pained expression on her mother's face. "Don't worry Mama; she probably won't stay long. You know how bored she'll get. She's used to having her social group around." Putting her arm around Sherry, she hugged her.

Sighing, Sherry said, "I know, but you know how condescending she can be. She'll do her best to make us miserable. I just hope she doesn't start harping about going back to Mobile with her." Last night before going to bed she had discussed staying at the farm with Rachel. They both felt it was the right thing for them. Like Rachel, Sherry had been wondering what direction her life was going in. Ever since she was a little girl she had always done exactly what her mother had wanted. Barbara had come from an old Mobile family, with enough money that she had never wanted for anything. Sherry always suspected money was the reason her parents fought so much. But unlike Barbara, Sherry had learned that money couldn't buy happiness or self-respect. Both were things that Sherry felt she was ready to find without her mother's interference. Looking back, Sherry could see that Darlyn had made the right choice by living with their father. Unfortunately at the time of her parent's divorce, Sherry was too young to make that choice for herself. By the time she was old enough to decide, she was too caught up in the exciting and never boring social circle that her mother insisted she be a part of. But now she was bored with the country club lifestyle. Even the Mardi Gras Society that she belonged to was so superficial she had not attended the last ball. Sherry was having some of the same feelings Rachel was experiencing, and she was relieved Rachel had decided not to marry Jason—his was not a lifestyle her daughter would have been happy with.

Separating in the upstairs hallway and going to their rooms, they each took their time getting cleaned up for dinner.

*   *   *   *   *

Rachel had definitely taken her time dressing for dinner. She knew her grandmother would not be happy if she came downstairs in a pair of jeans, a tee shirt and no shoes. Carefully selecting a pale blue silk pantsuit and a matching pair of low-heeled dress sandals, she looked at herself in the mirror. Not wanting to do anything with her hair, she brushed it dry and fluffed it so that it looked styled even though it wasn't. That was the advantage of being able to afford a decent haircut. The only makeup she ever wore was a light dusting of powder and some mascara.

Realizing she was stalling, she left her room and made it to the top of the stairs. Both Sherry and Rachel were tired from the long day they'd had, and the last thing Rachel wanted was for

Grandmother to start something with Sherry. She had always been the buffer between the two, but tonight she didn't feel up to the part. Hoping to make it downstairs before her mother she hurried down the stairs.

Reaching the bottom of the stairs and opening the sliding door to the parlor she saw that she was too late; her mother and grandmother were waiting for her. Barbara spoke before she could. "Good gracious child! I know I taught you how to descend stairs. You are not a hooligan that has run wild all your life. A true lady descends gracefully as if she's floating on a cloud, no matter how much of a hurry she is in!"

Feeling the full brunt of the reprimand Rachel said as contritely as she could, "I'm sorry, Grandmother, it won't happen again."

"Yes, well, see that it doesn't. Now come give Grandmother a kiss and say hello to our guest. I believe you know Mr. Newcume."

Turning, Rachel saw that her mother and Mr. Newcume had been witnesses to what had just occurred. Blushing, she stepped forward and kissed her grandmother's cheek and then her mother's. Finally she spoke to Mr. Newcume as she extended her hand in welcome. "How are you this evening, Mr. Newcume?" Unable to explain her feelings toward the man she withdrew her hand from his almost immediately.

Red-faced at having witnessed the reprimand that Rachel had received from her grandmother, he said, "Please ladies, call me Oscar." Smiling charmingly at all of them he tried to break the air of tension that had suddenly developed in the room.

Sherry came to his rescue by asking, "Tell us Oscar, what brings you over this evening? You are all dressed up; did you have a dinner date?"

"Why no, Ms. Sherry—I had a late meeting in Evergreen with my lawyer. I just stopped by on my way home to see if you ladies needed me to send a couple of my workers over to give you a hand at the chicken house tomorrow."

Seeing the spark in Sherry's eyes when she looked at Oscar, Barbara spoke up, "Then you haven't had dinner yet?" As was her style she did not wait for him to answer; instead she continued, "Good, you can stay and be our guest...we should be eating momentarily."

Not happy with this new development in the evening, Rachel went to the low bar in the corner and started to pour herself a glass of wine. Just as she started to drink it, Dora came to the parlor door and announced that dinner was ready.

Rachel sat quietly through dinner, letting Sherry and her grandmother entertain Oscar. As usual, Dora served a full course meal, complete with strawberry cheesecake for dessert. Rachel hardly tasted anything or heard much of their conversation. Instead she took in her surroundings. Aunt Darlyn had not changed much in the formal dining room. It still held the huge antique dining table with matching china cabinet and buffet that had belonged to her great-grandmother on her grandfather's side. The wallpaper was a soft ivory with hunter green border along the ceiling. Matching green drapes hung over the floor length windows. A large bouquet of flowers graced the middle of the table. *Dora must have picked them from Darlyn's rose garden*, she thought. So engrossed in her own musings, she didn't hear her grandmother speaking until she felt everyone staring at her. "I'm sorry, Grandmother, what did you say?"

"I said, if you are through picking at your dessert I think we should retire to the parlor for some brandy. Don't you agree?"

Wanting to be alone for awhile, Rachel replied, "If you don't mind Grandmother, Mother, I need to take a look at Aunt Darlyn's records in the study. I'm sure the two of you can entertain Oscar without me." Not waiting for an answer, Rachel wiped her mouth on the Irish lace napkin and left the dining room.

Appalled at the lack of manners shown by her daughter, Sherry again extended the invitation to Oscar to join them in the parlor for some brandy. Not wanting to eat and run, Oscar accepted saying, "How can I refuse such a beautiful woman? By all means, let's adjourn to the parlor." Assisting both ladies from their chairs he took one on each arm and escorted them to the parlor.

Upon reaching the study, Rachel pulled both sliding doors shut and leaned against them. Still wondering why she had taken such an immediate dislike to the man, Rachel sighed and took a deep breath. *I'm just tired*, she told herself. Maybe if she got to know him a little better her feeling of distrust toward Oscar Newcume would go away. Too tired to evaluate her feelings any further, she dismissed them and set about her task.

As a teacher one of the first things Rachel learned to do was get familiar with her surroundings. Just as she had done in the dining room she now looked around the study. She immediately decided it was a warm and cozy room. Light wooden panels of oak covered the walls. To the right of the study doors bay front windows looked out onto the porch. To her left was a massive old desk that had belonged to her grandfather. A huge dark brown leather chair sat behind it. On the wall facing the door was another fireplace. A small matching leather sofa faced the desk, close to the fireplace, and a twin to the braided rug in the parlor covered the study floor.

Going to the desk, Rachel booted up the computer. Aunt Darlyn had always stayed on top of all the latest technical gadgets. The computer was another of her indulgences. Having taught basic computer skills to her class at the elementary school, Rachel was able to handle her way around a computer. When the computer asked for the password, Rachel laughed to herself. Knowing Aunt Darlyn as well as she did, she knew there was only one thing that Darlyn would have used for a password. It could be nothing but her favorite saying. After typing in 'hens rule' and hitting enter, the computer came to life.

Looking at the folders available Rachel could tell that Darlyn had spent many hours in front of the computer; where she had found the time was another story. Selecting the folder marked 'Farm accounts' Rachel explored it first. After studying the spreadsheets, Rachel could see that the egg production had dropped by twenty-two percent from last year. Going into the next worksheet in this folder she found a list of all the suppliers and the costs of running the farm. Although production was down Aunt Darlyn was still making a profit. Closing this folder and going back to the main menu she chose another folder. This one contained a list of all Aunt Darlyn's other assets. Not wanting to get into stocks and bonds analogy right then, she closed this folder and went into the next one, marked 'Miscellaneous'. It held a list of all the other responsibilities of running the farm, such as when to plant the garden and who did the maintenance on the tractor and other farm equipment. Laughing out loud, Rachel thought Aunt Darlyn was giving instructions directly to her.

Stretching, Rachel suddenly felt as if someone was watching her. She had not closed the drapes at the windows when she came into the study. Darkness had fallen many hours ago, and there was no moon out tonight. Telling herself she was being foolish she walked to the window and looked out. Even though she saw nothing outside she could not shake the creepy feeling that had come over her. Startled by a noise at the door, Rachel jumped and turned to see what it was. Standing in the doorway was Dora.

With a haughty look on her face Dora said, "I'll be going to bed soon, Ms. Rachel. Will you be needing anything before I close the kitchen for the night?"

When she was a child she had tried to sneak into the kitchen for a late night snack only to be reprimanded by her grandmother in the morning.

Dora had been with Barbara since Sherry was a teenager and was fiercely loyal to Barbara. Answering her, Rachel said, "No thank you Dora. You can go on to bed." Rethinking, she changed her mind and said, "Dora, wait a minute, please." Stopping, Dora turned around and waited to see what Rachel wanted. "Tell me, why did Grandmother come here? I mean she has always hated this place. Even after Grandfather died she wouldn't come to visit Aunt Darlyn."

Giving nothing away, Dora looked at Rachel and replied, "You'll have to ask her yourself, Ms. Rachel. It's not my place to say." With that she turned and walked down the hall to the downstairs bedroom located to the right of the kitchen.

Not surprised that she couldn't get an answer out of Dora, Rachel decided she had better get to bed herself. Walking back to the desk, she shut down the computer and turned off the light. In the hallway she saw only the upstairs hall light burning. She had spent longer going over the accounts than she thought, and everyone else had already retired for the night. As quietly as she could she made her way upstairs and down the hall to her bedroom, turning off the light as she went past.

Susan Weekley

CHAPTER THREE

Rachel was so tired when she went to bed that she fell asleep as soon as her head hit the pillow. Bad dreams followed each other all night so it was not a restful sleep. Abruptly she woke up; not sure if she had heard something or if her dreams woke her, she reached for her robe and got out of bed. With a glance at the clock she saw that it was only 1:45 in the morning. Fully awake, she decided to check downstairs and find out what the noise had been. She met Sherry and Barbara huddling in the middle of the hall. *They made the noise that woke me*, she thought, and asked them what was wrong.

Both of the women shushed her, and whispered that someone was downstairs. With Rachel in the lead all three slowly walked to the top of the stairs. A soft ray of light poured out of the study doors, and a low humming noise was coming from the room. Rachel softly whispered to the women to stay where they were and started down the staircase. She crept to the bottom, trying to be careful and praying that none of the boards would squeak. When she reached the last step she saw Dora sneaking up the hall with a small cast iron skillet in her hand. Signaling for Dora to stay back, Rachel peeked into the study but saw no one in the room, so she motioned for the others to come on down.

The light in the study was coming from the computer. The others followed her into the room, turning on the overhead light as they entered. When she reached the desk, Rachel looked to see what program was running. A strange series of cryptic letters and symbols flashed on the screen, and every few seconds a low hum or beep would come through the speakers. Not knowing what to make of this Rachel stopped the program and shut the computer down again.

"Is that what woke me from my beauty sleep?" Barbara asked.

"I'm afraid so, Grandmother."

To keep her mother from making a scene in the middle of the night, Sherry spoke up. "Rachel, please try to be more considerate of the rest of us when you use that thing. Shut it down when you use it in the future."

Rachel knew she had shut it down before she went upstairs, but not wanting to upset anyone any more than they already were she decided to keep her mouth shut. Tomorrow she would ask Ollie if he knew anything about the program that had been running. Rachel apologized for waking them up, ushered everyone out of the study and turned off the light. As discreetly as she could, Rachel slid to the front door and checked it; the door was slightly ajar. Quickly she shut and locked it, knowing for sure that someone had been in the house; Rachel realized she would have to report this to the sheriff.

Following her grandmother and mother back upstairs Rachel told them good night. She made her way to her bed in the dark room, crawled under the covers, and tried to go back to sleep. After tossing and turning for another hour she finally fell into a deep dreamless sleep.

The next day was Saturday. A soft rain had fallen sometime in the early hours of the morning, washing everything fresh and clean. When Rachel woke, she saw a bright ray of sunshine filtering into the room. She could hear birds chirping outside her windows. Realizing she had over slept she jumped from the bed, threw on some clothes, ran into the bathroom to brush her hair and teeth, and then rushed out of the room. Irritated with herself for sleeping late she slowed down at the top of the back stairs, hoping to sneak out of the house without anyone seeing her. She knew Ollie would be behind schedule and they would be at the chicken houses for most of the day now. Wondering when she would find time to contact the sheriff about last night, she entered the kitchen. Her thoughts of sneaking out of the house were in vain. Grandmother, Sherry and Dora were all in the kitchen having a late breakfast.

"It's about time you got up! I thought you were going to lie in bed all day!" her grandmother exclaimed.

In a final attempt to get out of the house as quickly as possible, Rachel kissed her grandmother and mother good morning, and started to explain that she was in a hurry. "Ollie need's me at the chicken coops," she said as she headed for the back door.

Sherry stopped her before she could get there saying, "But, Rachel, honey, Ollie isn't expecting you this morning. I agreed to let a couple of Mr. Newcume's workers come over and help for a couple of weeks. They arrived early this morning." Sherry saw the look on Rachel's face and gave a slight shake of her head, silently signaling her daughter to not start an argument in front of Grandmother Barbara.

At her mother's nod, Rachel sighed and said, "Okay, but I would like to go down after breakfast and check on them." When she sat down at the table, Dora brought her a cup of coffee. Rachel realized she was starving and filled her plate with a fried egg smothered in hot buttered grits. She stabbed one of Dora's homemade buttermilk biscuits with her fork, popped it open, and filled it with some fried ham. She savored the taste as the salty ham teased her taste buds.

Barbara addressed her again as she watched her granddaughter eat, "Rachel, now that you are free today I need you to drive me into Evergreen. I have a hair appointment with Roxanne at eleven. Sherry has other plans and can't take me."

Thinking this was the perfect excuse to go into town and talk to the sheriff, she didn't try to get out of doing it. Instead she said, "Of course, Grandmother, I don't mind taking you into town. It will give me a chance to do some window shopping and see if any new shops have opened."

Her grandmother laughingly replied, "Evergreen may be the county seat for Conecuh County, but it certainly isn't a metropolis big enough to have a decent dress shop. Why, I bet you can't find an outfit close to the one you wore last night anywhere near here."

"I don't know Grandmother, I might. Roxanne said they have an exclusive dress shop in Evergreen called Homespun & More. It specializes in designer dresses and accessories."

"Like I said; nothing decent to wear. It's probably some local seamstress pushing fashions from the eighties!" Still laughing Barbara stood up and said, "I'll be ready by ten thirty." Tugging on Rachel's tee shirt she added, "Do see that you change into something more appropriate before then." Barbara left the kitchen and headed toward the parlor.

Dora mumbled under her breath and removed Barbara's plate from the table.

Rachel and Sherry looked at each other in surprise at this unexpected arbitrary remark, causing Sherry to ask Dora to repeat what she said. With a look that dared a response, Dora repeated what she had said loud enough for Barbara to hear. "I said, she thinks she's fooling me—like I can't smell that cigarette in here!" Grabbing more dishes from the table she turned around and started cleaning the kitchen.

Sherry spoke with concern to Dora, "Is there something we should know, Dora?"

Her face flushed from her outburst, Dora replied, "It's not my place to say. You'll have to ask Ms. Barbara." The expression on her face made

Sherry realize asking any more questions would be useless. She would just have to wait until she could speak to her mother.

The old grandfather clock in the foyer chimed 10:00, making Rachel quickly finish her breakfast. Her visit to the chicken house having to wait until this afternoon she said, "I guess I'd better hurry and get dressed if I'm taking Grandmother into Evergreen." She thanked Dora for breakfast and started up the stairs to her room.

After a quick shower Rachel dressed in a simple spring green colored cotton dress with matching short sleeve sweater. A pair of tan sling-back sandals completed the outfit. Pleased with the casual but classy attire she went downstairs just as the clock struck 10:30. She found Barbara in the parlor waiting for her. Not saying a word but giving Rachel a look of approval, Barbara handed the car keys to her.

The ride from Owassa to Evergreen took about fifteen minutes. Occasionally Rachel would point out different old houses or landmarks and ask a question about it. Her grandmother's responses were always short. Sensing that Barbara had something on her mind, Rachel gave up trying to have a conversation and they drove the rest of the way in silence.

Rachel looked around to see if any changes had been made in the old town as they drove over the high curving bridge that would take them down the main street. To her left she could see the steeple to the church where Aunt Darlyn and Uncle Mack had been married. Stopping at the red light at the bottom of the bridge Rachel didn't see any noticeable changes. The town was split down the middle by a railroad track on her left. The old wooden train station still stood, proving either the town was not one to embrace progress with open arms, or it attempted to preserve historical sites. Rachel wasn't sure which characteristic was true of the town's leaders. On the right corner was the Merchants Bank building. It was only three stories but was the tallest building on the street. Next to it was a bookstore. Various other businesses continued down the street. Roxanne's beauty salon was on this side of the street just past the next light. The other side of the track also held businesses. There was an appliance store, a hardware store, and a John Deer tractor store.

When the light turned green Rachel drove down to the next intersection looking for a place to park. She found a parking space on the side street close to the front of the building. After stopping the engine she handed the keys back to her grandmother and they got out of the car. Waiting on the sidewalk for Barbara to catch up, Rachel noticed that her grandmother was starting to look her age.

At sixty-four Barbara had aged gracefully. She went to the beauty salon every Saturday morning and had her hair styled, wearing it short and puffed on the top. Rachel had teased her once saying that her hairstyle had gone out of fashion years ago. Barbara had retorted that at her age she was just glad she still had hair that could be styled. Today, taking a closer look at her grandmother, Rachel could see a few age spots on her face and arms. Grandmother's weekly tennis matches at the country club helped her keep her figure; however, years of smoking were taking a toll on her. Rachel had heard her having a coughing spell during the night. Was that what had Dora so upset this morning? Arms linked, they walked side by side down the sidewalk to Roxanne's shop.

They spotted Roxanne immediately upon entering the beauty salon. She was at the first workstation cleaning a set of combs and brushes. Rachel looked at Roxanne and again thought how beautiful she was. The small gap in Roxanne's front teeth reminded Rachel of actress/model Lauren Hutton. Roxanne was a natural honey-colored blond; about five foot six with a figure to die for. A few years ago Roxanne had installed a tanning bed at the salon and Rachel was sure Roxanne was taking advantage of it. A glowing tan showed beneath the few freckles on her skin. Smiling and saying good morning, Roxanne seated Barbara in the chair and asked her what she wanted done.

Still in a non-talking mood, Barbara briefly said, "The same thing I always get."

Roxanne placed the cape around Barbara's neck, and said, "Okay, let's get started." She lowered the chair to the sink behind her and started wetting Barbara's hair. Still standing next to her, Rachel decided that this would be a good time to get away.

"I have some shopping to do, so I'm going to leave for a little while. Where did you say that new dress shop was?"

"It's just down the side street, next to the sheriff's office," Roxanne said pointing in the direction where Rachel had parked the car.

With a 'thanks', Rachel left the beauty shop. At the corner she stopped long enough to look around. The city council had cleaned up this street, and pretty pots of daffodils and other spring flowers were placed at each storefront. The local barber was standing out front of his shop sweeping the sidewalk, waiting for customers. Rachel could see the sheriff's office on the other side of the street and the dress shop was just past it. Carefully crossing the street Rachel decided to see Jake first.

The sheriff's office was a large brick building with steps leading to the entrance. Once inside Rachel decided there was nothing surprising about the offices. A long counter separated the room in half. Behind the counter she could see desks where a couple of deputies were sitting. In the back of the room another counter held a large coffeepot and several cups. A metal door at the back of the room led to the jail cells. To the left was a small interrogation room with a large shatterproof window. The other two doors were restrooms. Jake's office was on the right side of the back room. It too had shatterproof windows on each side of the door. The blinds inside the office were open and Rachel did not see Jake inside.

A deputy stepped to the counter and greeted Rachel as she approached. "Good morning, ma'am, I'm Deputy Wheeler; can I help you with something?"

She introduced herself and said, "If Sheriff Brewer is around I need to see him. It's regarding my aunt." Rachel did not want to go into details with the deputy only to have to repeat everything to Jake.

The deputy replied, "No, ma'am, he's out on Interstate 65. There was a pretty bad accident out there about daylight. We've been giving the state boys a hand with it. He's still trying to round up some cattle that got loose from the eighteen-wheeler that jackknifed out there." His thumb pointing to the other deputy, he continued, "Sammy and me, we had to relieve Karen so she could go to lunch, otherwise we'd still be out there. The sheriff is probably gonna be tied up the rest of the day."

"I see," she sighed. "Well, may I leave him a message, Deputy Wheeler?"

"Sure; tell you what, since you said it was regarding Mrs. MacKinstry, I'll take it to him myself." He handed her a pen and note pad, and waited for her to write the message.

Quickly she wrote, *'Need to see you as soon as possible. Urgent. Call me at the farm'*. After signing her name she folded the note and handed it to the deputy. She thanked him for his help and left the office. Her next stop was the dress shop, just one door down.

A bell above the door tinkled as Rachel walked into 'Homespun & More'. Her first impression was of a very organized and planned boutique. Small displays of the fashions were tastefully done in the limited space of the building. She appeared to be the only person in the shop. Walking toward a rack marked petite, she was startled when a woman stood up and said, "Good morning, may I help you find something?"

"Oh, you startled me. I thought I was the only one here." With a laugh at herself for being so jumpy she continued. "Roxanne over at the beauty shop recommended your shop to me. I thought I would come see what you have."

"I'll have to remember to give Roxanne a discount the next time she comes in. Are you looking for anything in particular?"

"No, just looking."

"Well, let me show you what I have in your size. My name is Sara Lynch, what's yours?"

"Rachel Collier. Are you related to Mr. Lynch at the funeral home?"

"Yes, he's my uncle." Pausing she asked, "Are you Darlyn's niece? The one who inherited MacKinstry Farm?"

Rachel walked to the clothes rack. Replying that she was and changing the subject, she asked, "Are you the owner here?"

Sara smiled, realizing that Rachel did not want to discuss her aunt's death, and said, "Well, yes and no." The puzzled look on Rachel's face prompted further explanation. "I'm part owner. I handle the retail end of the business, my partner Christi Reynolds is the designer. That's one of her pieces you're holding right now."

A closer look at the pale pink skirt she was holding had Rachel deciding the design was quite cosmopolitan. The long skirt had a small rose-colored floral print running the length with sage colored leaves. "The quality of Christi's work is wonderful."

"A pale pink shell would look nice with that skirt. I'll go get one."

While Sara was selecting a top, Rachel continued to look at the clothes. She chose a lime green pantsuit, surprised to see that it also was by Christi.

"Why don't you go try them on?" Sara said, handing Rachel the top she had selected and pointing to the back of the store. "The dressing room is over there."

After trying on both outfits Rachel decided she was going to like shopping here. Both garments fit as if they were made specifically for her. She found Sara behind the counter waiting for her when she came out of the dressing room. "I love both of these—they fit beautifully. Christi does very professional work. I'd like to meet her sometime."

"She comes in every weekend. If you come back again I'm sure she'll be here."

Her purchases paid for, Rachel said good-bye to Sara and headed back to the beauty shop.

Rachel spotted her grandmother still under the hair dryer. Roxanne was in the back room putting towels into the washer. Taking advantage of this time to speak to Roxanne alone, Rachel walked to the back room. Roxanne saw Rachel approaching out of the corner of her eye. "She should be ready soon."

"I'm in no hurry; actually I was hoping to get a chance to speak to you alone."

Turning on the washer, Roxanne turned around with a concerned look on her face. "Okay, what's on your mind? Has Jake found out anything else?"

"Not that I'm aware of; I did go by to speak to him, but he wasn't in."

"So what's bothering you?"

Before answering she looked behind her to make sure Barbara was still under the dryer. Quietly Rachel told Roxanne about the possible break in last night.

Clearly upset, Roxanne asked, "Are you sure the door was locked? Maybe the wind blew it open."

"No, it was locked—I checked before I went to bed and I was the last one up. I also know that I shut the computer down correctly. Someone was in the house, but I don't know what they were looking for."

Roxanne could see Barbara lifting the dryer off her head behind Rachel, and nodded in that direction. "Shhh." Roxanne said. In a louder voice she quickly changed the subject. "I see you made some purchases at the boutique. Let's see what you bought."

Rachel removed one of the outfits from the bag, showing Roxanne her purchases. After one look at the skirt and blouse, Roxanne exclaimed, "Oh, they're by Christi! I knew you would like what they have to offer."

With a smile, Rachel replied, "I do and I will probably go back soon."

Peeking around Rachel, Barbara looked to see what Rachel was holding. "It's pretty, but it still isn't as good as a designer original like you usually wear," she replied sarcastically.

Taking offense, Roxanne spoke up for her absentee friend saying, "Ms. Barbara, I'll have you know that Christi studied under one of the top fashion designers in New York. She only gave up her professional career there to move here with her husband. He happens to be the local district attorney for the county."

"Humph; well, whatever." Indignantly, Barbara changed the subject and said, "Do you think you could finish my hair now? I'm ready to go back to the farm."

Both women knew that Barbara would never admit to being wrong about anything. Roxanne smiled and winked at Rachel for having got one over on Barbara. Guiding Barbara back to the styling chair Roxanne said, "Come on, let's get you finished."

Ten minutes later Rachel and Barbara were in the car and on their way back to the farm. Once again trying to have a conversation with her grandmother, Rachel commented, "Roxanne did a good job; your hair looks very nice."

As she patted her hair Barbara replied, "She didn't do anything different to it. I could have done this good myself. Probably should have and saved myself some money."

Rachel just shook her head and they drove home in silence.

Rachel noticed a man mowing the front lawn when she pulled into the circular drive in front of the farmhouse. At first she thought it was Ollie, but looking again she realized it wasn't. This man was smaller and looked a little older than Ollie. *He must be one of the workers Mr. Newcume sent over,* she thought. Rachel retrieved her package from the back seat and started to help her grandmother up the front steps. Irritated, Barbara pulled her arm away from Rachel and said, "I'm not helpless; I can manage walking up the steps by myself."

Not sure what to think of her grandmother's behavior, Rachel stepped back and let Barbara go up the steps alone. She quietly followed her into the house, thinking she would need to speak to her mother about Grandmother's mood. There was definitely something going on with Barbara and it worried Rachel.

Dora met them in the foyer, and wiping her hands on an apron she asked if she could get them anything. Barbara replied, "Yes, Dora, please bring me a cup of coffee in the parlor."

"Nothing for me, Dora, thanks," said Rachel, as she started up the stairs.

"Where are you headed off to?" her grandmother asked.

Rachel paused on the stairs and answered her grandmother, "I'm going upstairs to change clothes, and then I need to check on things down at the chicken coops. Did you need me to do something for you Grandmother?"

"No, no, go on and do what you need to do." With that Barbara walked into the parlor and sat down on the sofa.

Changing into her work clothes Rachel went down the back stairs to the kitchen. Not seeing Dora around, Rachel snatched a fresh baked chocolate chip pecan cookie off the cooling rack and walked out the back door. She nibbled on the cookie as she walked, enjoying the warm spring day. The sunshine felt good on her back and the soft breeze that blew in her face was just cool enough to keep the sun from being too hot. Finishing the cookie she walked into the chicken house.

Ollie met her as she came in. Greeting her he said, "Afternoon, Ms. Rachel, didn't expect to see you down here today."

"I came to see how things were going. Are the workers Mr. Newcume sent over able to keep up with the work?"

"Yes ma'am! He sent us two fine workers. Matter fact, we have almost all the eggs already collected. We were just about to head out for some lunch." Before Ollie could say anything else a very pretty young Mexican girl walked out of the bathroom, followed by a young man. With their dark hair and eyes, Rachel could tell by looking at them that they were brother and sister. Ollie introduced them to Rachel. "This is Maria and Juan Cortez, Ms. Rachel."

With a smile Rachel welcomed them to MacKinstry Farm. Turning back to Ollie she said, "I won't keep you long Ollie, but I need to ask you something before you leave for lunch."

Ollie said to Maria and Juan, "Why don't you two go on out to the truck; I'll be there in a minute." After they were outside Ollie looked at Rachel and asked, "What's up, Ms. Rachel?"

Seeing the worried look on Ollie's face, Rachel smiled and tried to get him to relax. "Nothing's wrong, Ollie, I just needed to know if you know of any program my aunt may have on the computer that would be running at night."

Ollie took off his cap, rubbed his head and burst into laughter. "That Ms. Darlyn, God rest her soul, she was always doing something funny!"

Annoyed, Rachel asked, "What are you talking about, Ollie?"

Still smiling, Ollie composed himself and replied, "Well about a year ago, I guess, Ms. Darlyn signed up to look for aliens."

"Aliens? Ollie, I don't understand."

"I don't rightly know all about it, but I do know that it has something to do with a study that one of them colleges out in California's doing. Ms. Darlyn said she had it fixed up so that it would come on at night; supposed to send out some kind of signals into outer space to try to talk to aliens. That's all I know."

Rachel pondered on Ollie's comment, thinking it was an outrageous statement for him to make about her aunt. Then Rachel remembered reading about a study being conducted by Berkley into the theory of other life forms in outer space. Rachel started laughing, thinking this study sounded just like something Darlyn would do. Looking at Ollie, she said, "You're right, Ollie, Aunt Darlyn was always doing something funny!"

Ollie placed his cap back on his head and asked, "Was that all you needed me for Ms. Rachel?"

"Yes...no, Ollie, who was the man I saw mowing the front lawn when I came home?"

"Oh, that's Guy Hicks. Ms. Darlyn hired him a few days before...well, ahh, she hired him as a gardener; said she just couldn't keep up with everything by herself."

Not wanting to keep him from his lunch any longer, Rachel said, "Oh, well I guess we could use him. You go on and get some lunch; I'm going to get started cleaning some of these eggs. I'll see you when you get back."

Nodding his head as a goodbye, Ollie went to join his new friends.

The cleaning room was too quiet so Rachel went to the wall behind the old couch and turned on the radio. Tuning to an 'Oldies but Goodies' rock station, she sat down and started to work. Egg cleaning was not hard work but it was tedious and smelly.

*   *   *   *   *

Singing along with the radio, Rachel did not hear the door down the hall opening or the soft footsteps behind her. She was leaning over the egg in front of her, inspecting it closely, when she was suddenly hit on the back of the head. Dazed, she started to get up and turn around, but before she could turn she was hit on the head again. Unconscious, she slumped forward, her head landing on the eggs she had just cleaned.

The man picked her up from the stool and pulled her by the arms down the long hallway to the last chicken coop. The mixture of smashed eggs and blood coming from the cut on the side of her head made him laugh. Half dragging and half carrying her, he left her laying on the floor toward the back of the coop between the rows of nests. Shooing chickens out of his way he walked to the back of the large room and turned off the ventilation fans. Careful not to leave any fingerprints on the controls or the door he left the same way he had come.

CHAPTER FOUR

Sherry looked through the windshield of the car at the deep blue sky, thinking how much she was enjoying the day with Oscar. He had picked her up shortly after eleven and they had taken a leisurely drive through the country. When Sherry asked Oscar where they were going he said it was a surprise. Driving north on Highway 31 toward the Sepulga River, Oscar turned left on the other side of the Travis Bridge. To Sherry's surprise a park had been developed along the bank of the river. Voicing her surprise she exclaimed, "Hey, this is wonderful! How long has this park been here?"

Pleased that he had surprised her, Oscar replied, "The County took over this area a few years ago. For a time we were having trouble with kids coming down here at night and doing drugs. The land used to belong to Old Lady Tanner, but when she died some of the county officials and local businessmen decided to clean it up and make something nice out of it. The ladies historical society held several fund raisers and we all came up with enough money to build the playground and picnic area. The county highway department sent over truckloads of sand to expand the river bank."

"Well, I must say, I'm impressed. I remember coming here as a little girl. Papa Joe would bring Darlyn and me down here every Sunday for a swim. It wasn't much more than a trail through the woods, and the trees were so close to the river that there wasn't much of a bank. I always loved coming here in the summer."

Parking the car under a very large old oak tree, they got out. Several other vehicles were in the parking lot. A few small children were playing on the swings while their mother watched from one of the picnic tables. A young couple was wading at the rivers' edge, while closer to the bridge, an old man was fishing with a cane pole.

Oscar walked to the back of the car, popped the trunk and removed a wicker picnic basket and a blanket. "I hope you don't mind. I thought we could have a picnic down by the water. It's such a beautiful day and all."

"This is the kind of day a picnic was made for," Sherry replied. Taking the blanket from him Sherry led the way to a shady area close to the river, but far enough away from the playground that the children would not disturb them.

After eating a lunch of fried chicken, potato salad, and homemade yeast rolls, Sherry started to put the containers back into the basket. Watching her, Oscar said, "You know I had my cook put some of her delicious carrot cake in there somewhere. Help yourself to some."

"I have a better idea; let's go walk off some of this fried chicken and potato salad first. Then I might have some room for cake."

Agreeing, he offered her a hand up and they started walking along the riverbank. Walking toward the bridge, Sherry said, "I guess I'm telling my age but, I remember when that bridge was wooden. Back during the depression my great-grandfather joined the PWA. The original wooden bridge was one of the bridges they built during that time. Of course, progress eventually caught up and in the sixties the county tore it down and put up this concrete bridge."

"In my opinion, progress isn't always a good thing. I think we are losing too much of our history a lot of times."

Sherry sighed, "I agree completely. Just imagine how much more scenic this park would have been if the original wooden bridge were still here."

Growing silent, Oscar picked up a rock at the rivers' edge and skipped it across the water. Playfully Sherry said, "I bet I can make one take more skips than you!"

Oscar gave her a sly smile and took her up on the bet. After five throws Sherry had made her rock skip four times to Oscar's three. Taking her in his arms he conceded to the winner, saying, "Okay, you win. What do I owe you?"

She smiled at his handsome face and said, "Another date."

"You got it," he replied and leaned down and kissed her on the cheek.

Secretly pleased with this show of affection, Sherry took him by the hand and they started back to their blanket. Glancing at her watch Sherry exclaimed, "Oh, my, I didn't realize it was already one-fifteen. I guess I better get back to the farm. Mother is probably driving Rachel crazy by now."

"You're sure you have to go back right now? It's not that late."

"Yes, I'm sorry but I do need to get back."

"Okay, but only if you promise to go horseback riding with me tomorrow."

"Where did you have in mind?"

"My place. I'll pick you up tomorrow afternoon about four. It shouldn't be too hot to go for a ride. How does that sound?"

"It sounds like fun! I'll be ready."

Together they put away the rest of the dishes and headed back to the car.

* * * * *

Lunch at the diner in Evergreen had taken longer than usual. The place had been packed with people who had been re-routed off the interstate, thanks to the accident that morning. Ollie, Maria, and Juan had to wait for almost twenty minutes before they got a booth. Now, as Ollie turned onto the lane to the chicken house, he was praying that Ms. Rachel wouldn't be mad at them for taking so long.

Getting out of the truck, Juan said, "I'm so full I can hardly move."

Maria replied, picking at her younger brother, "You better move or you'll be here after dark by yourself. Ollie and I are almost through with collecting the eggs from our coops. When our eggs are clean we're leaving. Isn't that right, Ollie?"

Ollie laughed joining in the frolicking, and said, "That's right, Juan; and by the way, didn't I tell you...you get paid per egg, so you better get a move on!"

Still laughing as he followed them into the chicken house, Juan said, "Yeah, and I fell off the turnip truck yesterday."

Behind Ollie and Maria, Juan knew by their sudden stillness that something was wrong. Eggs were smashed and broken all over one of the workstations.

Looking at the mess, Maria asked, "What do you think happened?"

Ollie walked over to the radio and turned it off before he responded. "I don't know, but I don't see Ms. Rachel anywhere. We better look for her." Seeing the blood on the floor beneath the table he added, "I sure hope she's not hurt!"

Splitting up, they each took a different chicken coop to search. Ollie and Juan joined up at the last chicken coop on the left wing in the main hall. Suddenly they heard a low mournful wail coming from the last coop. Taking off at a run toward the sound, they knew it was coming from Maria. The closer they got the louder her scream became.

Ollie and Juan were both stricken with fear as they threw open the door. Dead and dying hens and roosters lay everywhere. By the heat and the stillness in the room, Ollie knew the ventilation fans were off. Rushing toward the back of the chicken coop, Ollie turned on the fans. Juan found Maria as she came running out from one of the rows of nests. Speaking hurriedly in Spanish, Maria spoke to Juan. Motioning for Ollie to follow him, Juan started down the row. Together they found

Rachel, with blood oozing from her head and a large bruise on her face. Picking her up, Ollie ran back to the main room. He placed Rachel on the couch, turned to the others and said, "Maria, go get something to help me stop the bleeding. Juan, run to the main house and get help!" Without saying a word both of them took off to do as Ollie had instructed.

* * * * *

Oscar parked the car in front of the house and jumped out to open the door for Sherry. He linked her arm in his and started walking her to the front porch. Reaching the steps he turned to her and said, "I sure have enjoyed your company today, Sherry. I'm looking forward to our ride tomorrow."

"I've had a good time today too, Oscar." Smiling up at him Sherry wondered if she should kiss him good-bye. As if he was reading her mind Oscar gently pulled her into his arms and embraced her. The sound of someone running in their direction made them jump apart, like teenagers caught in their first kiss.

Juan hurried to Mr. Newcume when he saw him and Sherry standing in front of the house and called out to him, so frightened he did not realize he was speaking in Spanish.

Only comprehending part of what Juan was saying, Oscar said, "Whoa, slow down son, my Spanish is rusty; what are you so excited about?"

Juan took a deep breath, and began again, this time in English. "Come quick, Mr. Newcume, we need help!"

Finding her voice Sherry spoke to Juan, "What's wrong; is it Ollie? Is he hurt?"

"No ma'am, not Ollie, Ms. Rachel. Hurry please, call the doctor!"

"Rachel! Oh my God, what happened? Tell me, how bad is she hurt?" cried Sherry.

"We don't know what happened. Dead chickens are all over the place. Come on and you'll see!"

Sherry started to take off but Oscar caught her by the arm saying, "No, you go call the doctor like he said. I'll go check on her." Pushing Sherry toward the house, Oscar gave her no choice but to do it. Not waiting for Sherry to go inside, Oscar and Juan ran toward the chicken houses.

* * * * *

From the minute Jake's deputy had delivered Rachel's message, he could not get her out of his mind. Deciding to use his lunch hour to ride out to the farm, Jake was about two miles away when the radio dispatcher called him. "Yeah, Karen, this is

Sheriff Brewer, go ahead," he replied, wondering what was wrong now.

"Sheriff, we just got a 911 call from Mrs. Collier out at MacKinstry Farm. I don't know many details, but she was asking for an ambulance."

Immediately concerned, Jake said, "Did she say who the ambulance was for?" He could tell by the static on his radio that Karen was trying to respond to his question, but he was going out of radio range. It would be another mile before he could pick her transmission up again. He threw the radio down on the seat and sped up, thinking that he would be at the farm before he was back in radio range. When he pulled into the drive Jake could see Sherry running toward the chicken house. He pulled up just as she reached the door. Sherry heard the car and turned around, thinking it was the ambulance. Jumping out of his Blazer Jake rushed up to Sherry, asking, "What happened Sherry, who's hurt?"

"It's Rachel, I don't—" Not waiting to hear any more, Jake swung the door open and ran inside, with Sherry right behind him. Jake's quick look around did not miss anything. The blood splattered on the workstation sent a sharp pain of fear straight to his heart. At first Maria and Juan were the only ones he could see in the room. Maria was sitting on the side of the couch still trying to get the wound on Rachel's head to stop bleeding. He rushed over and, kneeling next to Rachel, he pulled the cloth away from her head to see how badly she was hurt. The bruise on her face made him angry, and the cut on the side of her head made the fear in his chest deepen. Softly, Jake asked Maria what happened.

"We don't know. We found her in one of the chicken coops like this. Someone put her there." Both worry and fear showed on Maria's face as she spoke to Jake.

Behind Maria, Sherry spoke to Jake. "How bad is it Jake?" He could tell she was trying to stay calm, but tears were sliding down her face.

"She's unconscious, Sherry; I won't know more until the paramedics get here." Turning to Juan he said, "Why don't you go up to the end of the drive and direct them down here."

"Sure, I'll get them here." With that Juan took off as fast as he could go.

Looking around Sherry realized that Ollie and Oscar were nowhere in sight. Afraid that something may have happened to them she asked, "Maria, where are Mr. Newcume and Ollie?"

Pointing down the left wing Maria said, "Mr. Newcume wanted to see where we found her."

His investigative responsibilities kicking in, Jake placed Maria's hand back on the cloth to continue applying pressure to the wound. "Which coop?" he asked. Knowing he needed to contain the crime scene as much as possible he waited for her answer.

"The last one," she said.

Jake hurried down the hallway leaving Sherry and Maria to take care of Rachel. Not prepared for what he saw, Jake stopped at the open door. Even though the fans were back on, the smell of ammonia almost knocked him down. The eerie feeling of death surrounded him as he stepped into the room. Carefully stepping over dead hens, Jake called out, "Ollie, where are you?"

Ollie heard the sheriff's voice and yelled back, "We're down here, Sheriff, in the back."

Jake followed the sound of their voices, and found them at the end of one of the rows. "Is this where you found her?" he asked. Ollie nodded his head. Wanting to keep the scene as clean as possible for the lab work that needed to be done, Jake said, "Ya'll come on out of here. Ollie, you start telling me what you know."

Wiping his face with a handkerchief, Oscar spoke up, "You don't have to ask me twice to get out of here!" as he proceeded out of the chicken coop. Ollie and Jake followed behind him. While they walked Ollie told Jake that Maria, Juan and him had gone to lunch and left Rachel alone in the chicken house.

Clearly upset, Ollie fought back the tears that kept coming to his eyes. "I shouldn't have left her here alone, not after what happened to Ms. Darlyn. It's my fault, Sheriff, I should have been here."

"It's not your fault, Ollie. What happened to Ms. Darlyn was an accident. You couldn't have known something was going to happen to Rachel."

"I left her cleaning eggs, Sheriff; there's nothing dangerous about that. Someone came in and hit her on the head, then left her in the coop to die with the chickens. They turned the fans off."

"Who turned the fans back on?"

"I did; we couldn't have stayed in there long enough to find her without them pulling some of the ammonia out of the room."

They walked back into the main room, and Jake said, "Okay, Ollie that's enough for now; you go on outside and wait for me." Ollie did as he was told.

Jake was surprised to see Oscar standing with his arm around Sherry, but did not say anything about it. Instead he said, "I'm gonna need to speak to each of you at some point about all this, so stay around."

At that moment they could hear the wail of sirens. Ollie stuck his head in the door and said,

"Ambulance is here Sheriff, and so is one of your deputies."

"Thanks, Ollie," was all Jake replied.

While the paramedics worked on Rachel, Jake spoke to Sherry and Oscar. They explained to him that they had just gotten home when Juan came and told them to get help. He was finished taking their statements by the time the paramedics had Rachel ready for transport.

Speaking to Sherry, one of the medics said, "She's stable enough now to take her to the hospital, Ma'am. Do you want to ride with us?"

Jake nodded at Sherry, indicating that he was through with his questions. Before he could say anything Oscar interrupted, asking, "Sherry, don't you think you need to let your mother know what has happened?"

"Oh, God, she's probably half way down here by now, what with the sirens and all! I better go talk to her." Addressing the paramedic she told him to go on and take Rachel to the hospital and that she would follow as soon as possible.

Taking Sherry's arm Oscar said, "Come on, I'm going with you." Thankful for Oscar's support Sherry nodded her consent and they started for the farmhouse.

The deputy that had arrived with the ambulance held the door open as the stretcher was wheeled out: the same deputy that Rachel had spoken to at the sheriff's office that morning. Coming inside, he walked up to Jake and asked what happened. Explaining what he knew so far, Jake instructed Deputy Wheeler to get the forensic team on scene and to keep a guard posted until further notice. Walking toward the door Jake said, "Charlie, I'm going to the hospital in case Ms. Collier wakes up. Let me know what you guys find as soon as you can."

"Sure, Sheriff, you know I will," responded the deputy.

Walking outside Jake saw Ollie, Maria and Juan standing beside Ollie's pickup. Jake spoke to them, making sure that they would stay and each give statements to the other deputies that would be arriving shortly, then climbed into his Blazer and headed into Evergreen.

* * * * *

Again watching from his hiding place behind the boulder, the man could see everything that had happened. He had been smug thinking that this job was over now that the younger woman was dead. Watching the ambulance pull away with the siren on, he knew she hadn't died yet. The boss was going to be even angrier with him and would not pay him as long as she stayed alive. Nothing about this job was going as planned, and now the sheriff was sticking his nose into the situation. He had killed the first woman, making it look like an accident, thinking that would be the end of it. But no, she had relatives that moved in. That was his boss's mistake, thinking the old lady didn't have any relatives. Shaking his head and thinking that maybe he would just leave and let the boss finish his own dirty work, the man eased his way back through the woods as quietly as he could.

Susan Weekley

CHAPTER FIVE

Jake reached the hospital a few minutes before Rachel's mother and grandmother, and spoke to Doctor Lowery alone. Standing outside of the examination room Jake asked, "What's her condition Doc? Is she awake...can I talk to her yet?"

The doctor removed his stethoscope and shook his head no, saying, "No Jake, she hasn't come around yet. She took a pretty nasty hit on the head. We've stopped the bleeding and stitched up the wound. But she has a concussion, and we're going to be keeping a close eye on her for a day or so." Seeing the concern on Jake's face Doctor Lowery continued, "Take it easy, son, she's going to be all right. There is no sign of brain damage and no broken bones. Her lungs looked okay—no permanent damage from the ammonia fumes—but her voice may be hoarse for a while. You can go in with her if you want."

"Thanks, Doc. Her mother and grandmother should be here soon. I'd like to have a few minutes alone with her first. Maybe she'll wake up and I can ask her what she remembers."

"She might, but she might not. Sometimes with a concussion the patient doesn't remember things right away. She'll probably be disoriented for a while."

Jake opened the door and went into the room, nodding his head showing that he understood. Seeing Rachel lying in the hospital bed almost took Jake to his knees. She looked so small and helpless that all he wanted was to take her in his arms and keep her safe. Not sure where these feelings were coming from, he walked to the side of the bed and gently touched the bruise on the side of her face. Without realizing it, he started talking to her. "You're gonna be all right, baby. I'm not going to let anything ever happen to you again. Wake up, sweetheart. Let me see those beautiful green eyes. Come on Rachel, talk to me, yell at me, anything, just wake up, baby." Running a hand through his hair he tried to keep his emotions under control, but he couldn't. He reminded himself he had to stay focused on his job and not get involved with

Rachel, but realized it was useless. His heart was breaking seeing her like this.

*   *   *   *   *

Moaning, Rachel fought to wake up. Her head hurt so bad that all she wanted to do was sleep, but she could hear someone's voice telling her to wake up. Turning her head in the direction of the voice she slowly opened her eyes. Finally, Jake's face came into focus. Looking around the room she knew that she was in a hospital. She was confused, thinking her mind was playing tricks on her. She could have sworn someone had called her 'baby' and 'sweetheart', but after the way she had treated the sheriff she knew it wasn't him. Suddenly remembering what happened she tried to sit up, but dizziness overtook her and she carefully lay back down. Touching the bandage on the side of her head, she looked at Jake and with a raspy voice asked, "How did I get here?"

Relief flooded through him, and taking her hand in his he smiled at her. After a minute he stood up and answered her question. "We brought you here in an ambulance. Do you remember anything that happened?"

Trying hard to remember she said, "All I remember is that I was working in the chicken house cleaning the eggs and something hit me on the head."

"You didn't see anyone at all, or hear anything before you were hit?"

"No, I was singing along with the radio and didn't hear anything."

Before Jake could ask her any more questions the door to the room flew open and in marched Barbara, followed by Sherry. Covering up her feelings by trying to appear in control of the situation, Barbara looked at Jake questionably and said, "I see she is awake; has she told you what happened?"

Taking pity on Jake, Rachel interjected with a weak voice, "I don't know what happened Grandmother. I've told the sheriff all I can remember."

Not satisfied with this, Barbara gave Jake a stern look and replied, "Well, if she has told you all she knows, don't you think you need to be out looking for who did this, instead of standing here?'

*   *   *   *   *

Jake was not intimidated in the least by Barbara, but he did have work to do so he smiled at her and said, "Yes, ma'am, I do. But I needed to see if maybe she got a look at the person who did this to her. A description of the person would help me find him sooner, you know." Still smiling he started for the door. Stopping, he turned toward Rachel and said, "I'll be back to check on you later." Motioning for Sherry to follow him, he stepped into the hall. When she came out of the room, Jake told her that he would be posting a guard in the hall for Rachel's protection. He already had one at the farm to keep an eye on things there. Thanking him, Sherry went back into the room.

Starting down the hall Jake ran into Oscar sitting in the waiting room. He jumped up as the sheriff came into the room and asked, "How is she doing, Jake?"

Jake answered his question, looking at him suspiciously. "Doc Lowery says she's going to be fine." Deciding now was as good a time as any to question Oscar about his association with the Collier woman, Jake continued, "How long have you known Mrs. Collier, Oscar?"

"I just met her two days ago. Why, Jake, you don't think I had anything to do with any of this, do you?"

"I don't know what to think at this point, but I have to ask questions to be able to find out what's going on! So don't start getting defensive on me!"

Calming down, Oscar said, "I know...I'm sorry, Jake, I'm just worried about Sherry, that's all." Seeing the look of disbelief on Jake's face, Oscar continued. "I've known her for all of two days, Jake, but she means more to me than I can say. Not since my wife died have I enjoyed being in a woman's company like I do hers."

Jake backed off, recognizing some of his own feelings in what Oscar was saying. "I got work to do; why don't you help keep an eye on things here and let me know if Rachel remembers anything?" Not waiting for a response Jake left the hospital.

Driving in the direction of the farm Jake got angrier by the minute. He knew he would have to find the person responsible for this as soon as possible. What he needed was someone with experience to talk to. Turning off Highway 31 onto a dirt road Jake headed toward his Uncle Russell's cabin in the woods. Hunting season was over, but he knew his uncle would be fishing at the lake.

* * * * *

The afternoon had been busy, but Jake was still no closer to finding the person who had attacked Rachel or the reason why she was attacked. After leaving his uncle at the lake, Jake had gone to the farm to check on the progress there. The forensic team had finished and was leaving by the time he reached the farm. Jake told them to rush their report and have it on his desk first thing in the morning. The only fingerprints that were found were Ollie's on the fan switch; the weapon used to hit Rachel was never found. Making sure that Deputy Wheeler would be there all night to guard the scene, Jake told him that he was going back to the hospital.

Darkness was falling as Jake reached Evergreen. Stopping at the florist shop on Main Street, Jake caught the florist before she closed up for the night. Picking out a bouquet of pink carnations, Jake headed for the hospital.

Feeling self-conscious carrying the flowers, Jake spoke to the deputy posted at the door, saying, "How's everything going here, Sammy?"

"Mr. Newcume made her mother and grandmother leave a few minutes ago to go eat some dinner. She's by herself right now, Sheriff."

"No other visitors?"

Grinning, Sammy looked at what Jake was holding and replied, "No, just a few flowers delivered this afternoon, but the nurses took them in."

Giving the deputy a 'go to hell' look, Jake went into the room. Afraid she may be asleep Jake pushed the door closed as quietly as he could. Turning around he saw that not only was Rachel awake, but she looked better. Some of the color was coming back to her face. The bruise on the right side of her face still looked bad, but he knew it would be gone in a few days.

Smiling wasn't easy but Rachel tried her best to show Jake that she was happy to see him. "Are those for me?" she asked. The only response she got from Jake was a nod. "Do I look that bad? You could come closer, you know; that way I won't have to strain my voice to make you hear me."

Jake realized he had been staring, cleared his throat and said, "Ah, sorry—you look better than you did earlier today. I'm glad." He stepped closer to the bed, stopped and looked around the room.

Figuring out that Jake was looking for a place to put the flowers, Rachel said, "Why don't you hand those to me? I can get the nurse to bring in a vase for them later."

He handed the flowers to Rachel, pulled up a chair and sat down. Jake again looked around the room trying to think of something to say. Sammy had been right—several flower arrangements had been delivered that afternoon. Waving his hand in that direction he said, "You must have made a few friends in the short time you've been in Evergreen. Who all sent you flowers?"

"I'm not sure who sent all of them. The roses by the window are from Mother and Grandmother. The sunflowers are from Roxanne. I don't know about the other two."

Walking over to the arrangements, Jake pulled the cards from each of them and handed them to Rachel, saying, "Here, read the cards."

She tried to show no emotion as she opened the first one, but Jake could see a worried look in her eyes. After reading the second card Rachel looked puzzled.

Jake felt a twinge of jealousy stirring in his heart, thinking they might be from a boyfriend or lover. Keeping his thoughts to himself he said, "Mind if I ask who they are from?"

"Not at all," she said, "The first one was from Mr. Newcume. The second one I'm not sure who he is. I guess they could have been brought in here by mistake."

Taking the cards from Rachel, Jake read them. The first one was from Oscar just as Rachel had said. Setting it aside he read the second card. They had been sent from Alec Jamison. Jealousy flared a spark again, and angrier than he intended Jake said, "It's from Jamison's Feed Company. When did you meet him?"

Surprised by the anger in Jake's voice, Rachel flashed him a look of anger back and said, "I haven't. Who is he?"

Again making a mental note to pay Mr. Alec Jamison a visit, Jake hid his anger and explained to Rachel that Jamison Feed Company was who she bought the chicken feed from.

Relaxing Rachel said, "Oh, well I guess I'll have to be sure to thank Mr. Jamison for the flowers as soon as I get out of here."

Before Jake could say anything else, there was a knock at the door. Sherry, Barbara and Oscar filed into the room.

Surprised to find Jake in the room, Sherry asked if he had any news on Rachel's attacker. Jake stepped away from the bed to make room for Rachel's family, and told them that nothing new had come up.

Barbara walked to the chair that Jake had vacated and sat down, saying, "Then why are you here?"

Appalled at her grandmother's rudeness, Rachel gasped, "Grandmother, he's doing his job! Don't be so hard on him!"

"Humph, by the sound of your voice he's been making you talk too much. You need your rest, young lady!"

Sherry interjected, trying to stop this conversation from turning into an argument. "Your grandmother is right, Rachel you do need to get some rest, so we're going to leave you now."

"I'm not leaving; Oscar, you will take Sherry home, won't you?" replied Barbara.

Thinking he would like nothing better than to spend some more time alone with Sherry, Oscar said, "Of course I will, Ms. Barbara."

"Fine, then why don't all of you clear out of here? I'll keep Rachel company tonight."

Speaking up, Jake said, "It's not necessary for any of you to stay the night; I have a deputy posted outside. No one will be coming in here without his say so."

Not changing her mind, Barbara said, "Well then we'll both be safe, won't we? Now tell Rachel good night."

Taking their cue to leave, Sherry kissed her daughter good-bye, saying to Barbara, "I'll be back first thing in the morning." Looking at Rachel she said, "I'll bring you some clean clothes, okay baby?"

Rachel yawned and said, "Okay, I'll see you in the morning. Oh, Mama, make sure Dora feeds the kitten, won't you?" Closing her eyes, she dozed off.

Quietly Jake, Sherry and Oscar left the room. Pulling the deputy off to the side, Jake watched Sherry and Oscar leave the hospital. Speaking to Deputy Phillips, Jake said, "Make sure no one except medical personnel comes in here; understand, Sammy?"

Not taking the remark personally Sammy said, "Of course, Sheriff; no one comes in without my approval."

Jake left the hospital and started home. He was tired, and knowing that he had a busy day tomorrow, he wanted to get some sleep. He planned to get up early and drive to Andalusia to see Mr. Alec Jamison.

* * * * *

The next day had started out overcast with the threat of rain, but so far the storm had not come. Jake's mood wasn't much better. Leaving Evergreen at seven that morning he drove to Andalusia hoping to catch Mr. Jamison in his office. It was only a thirty-minute drive, but when he got to Andalusia, the secretary at Jamison Feed Company informed him that Alec had already left to make a delivery outside of Greenville. Driving back to Evergreen, Jake decided to stop by the hospital and check on Rachel before going into the office. Maybe if she remembered something that might help he wouldn't feel like he had wasted the whole morning. It was still early when he reached the hospital and there were plenty of parking spaces. Parking close to the entrance he walked briskly inside.

Deputy Phillips was still standing guard in the hallway. Speaking to him Jake said, "Good morning, Sammy; everything go all right last night?"

Stretching Sammy replied, "Yeah, boss, everything was quiet. Hey, I saw your uncle up here last night. He offered to relieve me long enough to take a smoke break. I hope that was all right; I mean he used to be the sheriff and all."

Thinking that his uncle was checking up on him after their talk yesterday afternoon, Jake just shook his head yes and said, "Why don't you go get some breakfast? I'm gonna be here for a while."

"I've had breakfast, Sheriff, but I could use some coffee." Starting down the hall the deputy added, "I won't be long."

Knocking as he entered Rachel's room, Jake was surprised to see Sherry there so early. She must have been there for a while, because Rachel was no longer wearing the hospital gown she'd had on yesterday. Instead she had on a very expensive cream colored nightgown and matching robe. Small, embroidered butterflies and flowers ran up the front of the robe. Instead of making Rachel look more childlike, the nightgown and robe made her look very feminine. The attraction Jake felt toward Rachel at that moment was so strong he again found himself having to fight the urge to rush to her side and wrap his arms around her. Getting control of his feelings, he stood just inside the door. No one seemed to notice he had come in.

Doctor Lowery was also in the room standing on the opposite side of the bed from Sherry. Feeling tension in the air, Jake looked from one to the other. Before he could ask what was wrong Doctor Lowery said to Sherry, "I'm sure it's nothing to worry about. She was on a very strong medication last night. She was just dreaming."

Clearly upset, Rachel interrupted the doctor saying, "Well, if it was a dream it was very real!"

A movement at the window made Jake notice Barbara for the first time. He had forgotten that she had spent the night. Walking to the side of the bed Barbara took Rachel's hand and tried to calm her down. "Rachel, honey, I was here all night; the only person who came into the room was the night nurse." Pausing for a moment she continued, "She did favor your Aunt Darlyn, but I can promise you it wasn't her. Like the doctor said, the medicine made you think it was Darlyn."

Not ready to believe her grandmother either, Rachel still persisted, "But she was here, and she told me I was going to be all right. She told me not to worry because she was looking out for me!"

"That's right, honey, the nurse told you that. I heard her." Patting Rachel on the shoulder as if she were a child, Barbara walked back to the window and looked outside.

Jake made his presence known by clearing his throat. He hated seeing Rachel in such a state and wanted to put his arms around her and comfort her, but there were too many people in the room. Seeing the sheriff standing there the doctor made his exit, leaving Jake to handle the situation. Wanting to be alone with Rachel, Jake said, "Sorry to interrupt ladies, but might I talk to Rachel alone for a few minutes? Ms. Barbara, you look like you could use a break."

Barbara agreed with Jake, and said, "You're right, Sheriff, I think I'll take a walk outside before the storm breaks." Turning she looked at Sherry and said, "Come, go with me, Sherry. The sheriff will take care of Rachel while we're gone."

Barbara instructed Rachel to try to rest, and followed Sherry out the door.

Before Jake could say anything, Rachel gave him a look that dared him to deny it, and said, "I know you heard most of that. You probably think I'm nuts too."

Sitting on the side of the bed, Jake just smiled at her and said, "I'd probably be seeing things too, if I had taken as bad a knock on the head as you did."

Finally feeling as if someone was listening to her, Rachel gave Jake a small smile back and said, "Is this a social call, or have you found out who hit me?"

With a sigh Jake said, "I haven't found out anything new. I was hoping maybe you had remembered something else about yesterday."

"Like I told you, the only thing I know is that I got hit. I didn't see who did it or hear anything that may have been a clue." Grinning wickedly at Jake, Rachel said, "But I do remember one thing that happened yesterday."

Getting Jake's full attention, he waited for her to continue. When she didn't say anything else but kept grinning at him he gave in and asked, "Okay, what do you remember?"

"Oh, just that a certain someone called me 'baby' and 'sweetheart'. Tell me, do you really think my eyes are beautiful?" she teased.

Two can play this game, Jake thought and leaned toward her, looking into her eyes, "I'm not sure, I can't decide what color green they are. They aren't the color of emeralds, and they are not the color of jade." Looking closer than he intended Jake was suddenly drawn toward her. It took him a minute to realize she had suckered him in. Pulling him closer she brushed her lips against his.

Electricity shooting through his body, he gently gathered her into his arms and kissed her back.

Hearing a knock at the door, Jake immediately stood up and said come in. Expecting it to be Sherry and Barbara, Jake was surprised to see Alec Jamison standing in the doorway.

Thinking the man must be in the wrong room, Rachel was curious when Jake shook hands with the man and asked him to come in. Intrigued by this stranger, Rachel sat up to get a better look at him. He was about the same height as Jake, but not as muscular; actually, he was a little on the skinny side. Attractive as this man was with his blond hair and blue eyes, Rachel thought he was too much of a pretty boy—she liked her men a little more rugged. Although her voice was still a little raspy, Rachel asked Jake to introduce her to the man.

"I'm sorry, I forgot you two haven't met. Rachel Collier, this is Alec Jamison—"

"Oh, so you are the one who sent me the flowers. They are lovely. It was very thoughtful of you, Mr. Jamison," she said, cutting Jake off in mid-sentence.

"It was no trouble Ms. Collier, I thought it was the least I could do, what with you just losing your aunt and all."

Trying to divert some of Alec's attention away from Rachel, Jake asked Alec how he knew about

Rachel's accident. He had made sure that the attack had not been reported to the newspaper before he left the farm yesterday.

Alec answered Jake's question, "I went by the farm yesterday afternoon to ask Ollie when he would need another feed delivery. He told me about the accident." Looking at Rachel he said, "I sure am sorry about all this; Ollie told me about losing a lot of chickens and that you probably would not need as much feed as you had been ordering."

No one had told Rachel where she had been found. Confused, Rachel asked, "Losing a lot of chickens? What do you mean?" Waiting for an answer she looked from Alec to Jake.

Finally, Jake answered saying, "Rachel, after you were hit on the head, whoever did it put you in one of the chicken coops and turned off the ventilation fans. That's why your voice is so hoarse. The fumes affected your lungs and vocal cords."

"What?!" she gasped.

In an effort to reassure her, Jake continued, "Doctor Lowery said the ammonia didn't do any permanent damage. That's the main thing!"

Sighing, Rachel asked if either of them knew how many chickens were lost. Both of the men shook their heads no.

Deciding now was a good time to leave, Alec said, "Well, I guess I better get going. I've still got work to do." Starting for the door he said, "It was nice finally meeting you Ms. Collier. I'm sure I'll be seeing you again soon."

"I'm sure you will. I plan on being out of this place soon and back home. It was a pleasure meeting you, Mr. Jamison."

"Please call me Alec," he said smiling brightly at her.

"Only if you'll call me Rachel," she said returning the smile.

"Good-bye, Rachel." Nodding at Jake, he said, "Sheriff," and walked out the door.

Jealousy flashing in Jake's eyes, he looked at Rachel and said, "I don't want you talking to him without someone else being around."

Coyly she responded, "Why, Jake, I think you may be jealous."

Caught in the act, Jake lied. "No I'm not. I just want you to be careful until I figure out what's going on."

Not believing Jake for a minute, Rachel thought about what he said. After a moment she replied, "Maybe you're right. We don't know who is responsible for what's been happening. I promise I'll be careful."

Relieved that she did not argue with him, Jake leaned over and kissed her on the cheek. "Thank you. I guess I'd better be going for now too. I'll check on you later. Okay?"

Settling back on the bed she said good-bye to Jake. After he left she dozed back off into a peaceful sleep just as the storm finally hit.

CHAPTER SIX

Even though Barbara and Sherry forbade her from leaving her bed, the day after coming home Rachel slipped out of the house to see how things were going in the chicken coops. She found Ollie, Juan and Maria removing the last of the dead chickens and taking them to the incinerator behind the chicken house. Years ago the dead chickens had been dumped in a deep hole at the far end of the property and left to rot. Remembering that, Rachel could still smell the foul scent of decaying birds. Now, due to the changes made by the Federal Environmental Agency and the county health department all dead animals had to be cremated. Questioning Ollie on the loss, she was relieved to find out that only about 2000 of the hens and 40 of the roosters had died. Deciding the loss was minimal, Rachel returned to the house. Somehow she managed to sneak back upstairs and into her room without being missed. After a couple more days in bed she could stand it no more and put her foot down with her mother and grandmother. Reluctantly, they agreed to let her get back to work. The next two weeks went by without any more trouble.

Rachel had been released from the hospital the day after she kissed Jake. Although he had called a few times to check on her she had not seen him since. Not sure if Jake was busy on the case or if he was avoiding her, Rachel decided to keep herself busy and put him out of her mind. Every night she would go in the study and record the day's events in the computer, and update the farms daily profits. Following the daily schedule Darlyn had left, Rachel realized they were behind on planting their garden. She told Ollie that they would get started on it over the weekend.

Saturday morning dawned warm and sunny. Temperatures were supposed to be in the high seventies, so Rachel dressed in shorts and a tee shirt. Finally locating her tennis shoes under the bed she went down for breakfast. Rachel was surprised to see Molly in the kitchen with Dora.

Seeing Rachel enter the kitchen Dora asked if she was ready to eat. Pouring herself a cup of coffee Rachel said, "Sure, Dora, whenever you have it ready."

Rachel leaned against the counter watching Molly play with the kitten. She was sitting on the floor, pulling a piece of yarn across her leg, making the kitten jump as he chased the string.

Dora explained why Molly was there, and handed Rachel a plate of steaming hot blueberry pancakes. "The daycare isn't open on the weekends. She usually stays with Roxanne on Saturdays but Roxanne has a wedding party coming in this morning and she couldn't watch Molly. And of course your grandmother wouldn't change her appointment to another day. I told Ollie that I would watch Molly; she can keep me company today." As if the lengthy explanation had exhausted her, Dora sighed and turned back to the stove.

Amazed that Dora said so much at one time, Rachel sat down to eat, watching Molly as she ate. Feeling Rachel watching her, Molly left the kitten and came to the side of the table. At first she just stood there watching Rachel eat. Taking a piece of bacon and putting it on a napkin Rachel slid it over in front of Molly. Pretending not to watch, Rachel wondered if Molly would eat it. Molly's large dark eyes looked from the bacon to Dora and back to the bacon. Slowly she reached for the bacon. Just before she picked it up, Dora caught Molly's hand, saying, "Oh, no you don't! You have to wash your hands before you can eat, little lady." Tickling Molly, Dora explained about kitten germs, and that she should always wash her hands after playing with him. Giggling Molly came back to the table and ate her bacon. Her eyes still shining brightly from laughter Molly exclaimed, "Dora's making cookies! She's gonna let me help!"

Smiling at the excitement on the child's face Rachel asked, "What kind?"

Molly appeared to think about this, but not knowing the answer she turned and yelled at Dora, "What kind?"

Drying her hands on a dishtowel Dora looked at the two and replied, "Gingersnaps." Changing the subject she took Molly by the hand and said, "But that will be later; why don't you take the kitten outside to the swing for a while?"

Molly ran across the room, gathered the kitten in her arms, saying "Okay!" and headed toward the back door.

After helping her outside Dora commented, "That child's a pistol! Won't eat a thing unless she can stand up. She's just like her daddy, always on the go." Taking dishes off the table to the sink, Dora went back to work. Rachel could see her occasionally peeking out the window above the sink, watching Molly.

Still amazed at how much Dora had spoken but not commenting, Rachel finished her pancakes. Thanking Dora for breakfast she left to go find Ollie.

She found him in the old barn. He was supposed to be getting the tractor ready to begin plowing, but instead he was talking to someone. Stepping inside the barn Rachel recognized the man. It was the gardener, Guy Hicks. As soon as Rachel got close Guy looked at Ollie and said, "I got work to do, see you later." Without speaking to Rachel at all he walked out of the barn.

Stunned by Guy's rudeness, Rachel asked, "What was that all about?"

Shrugging his shoulders Ollie commented, "That's just Guy. He don't have much to say to anyone."

"Well, what was he doing in the barn?"

"He only came to put the gardening shears back where they belong," Ollie answered, pointing to the shears hanging on the wall.

Dismissing the gardener from her mind, Rachel asked Ollie if he was ready to get started. His cap in one hand and the other running through his hair, Ollie asked how big a garden she had planned.

Rachel explained, "According to Aunt Darlyn's notes we should plow the other side of the field this year."

Ollie replaced his cap on his head and rephrased his question, "Okay, what are you planting? Are you wanting a large garden?"

"Not this year. I checked the freezer and there are still a lot of vegetables from last year. I thought maybe a couple rows each of some corn, field peas, butter beans, squash, okra and tomatoes would be enough. Oh, and maybe some watermelons and peanuts."

"Sounds good to me, let's get started." Ollie helped Rachel load bags of seed onto a flat bed trailer and then he hooked it to the back of the tractor. With Rachel riding on the back of the trailer they rode out to the field. The garden was on the opposite side of the house, away from the chicken coops.

The morning had started off good, and they were almost half way through with planting the garden. Ollie was driving the tractor, pulling a disc to plow up the soil. Rachel followed at a safe distance behind throwing seeds into a row of the freshly turned earth. The sun was getting hotter and sweat was pouring off both of them. Straightening up and stretching her back muscles, Rachel took off her straw hat to wipe the sweat from her forehead. As she did this she noticed Ollie climbing off the tractor and walking toward her. Thinking he wanted to take a break she wondered why he had not turned the tractor off.

When he reached her, Ollie yelled over the sound of the tractor, "We have a small problem, Ms. Rachel."

"What kind of problem?" she yelled back.

"I don't think this side of the field has ever been plowed before. There is an old property post in the ground just ahead of the tractor. We're gonna have to dig it up before we can finish plowing."

"Show me what you are talking about, Ollie," she yelled over the tractor again.

Walking back to where he had been working, Ollie stopped and turned the tractor off. Together they walked in front of the tractor to the old property post.

Logically thinking on this situation, Rachel asked, "Wouldn't it be easier to try and pull it out of the ground instead of digging it up?"

"Pull it out with what?"

Pointing to the top of the post Rachel said, "See that hook at the end of the post— couldn't we attach a rope to it and tie the other end to your pickup and then pull it out of the ground?"

Taking off his cap and wiping sweat from his face, Ollie pondered on this idea for a minute or two. Finally replacing his cap, he said, "Guess it might work. I'll go get some rope and the pickup."

While Ollie was gone Rachel walked to the edge of the field and sat down under an oak tree out of the sun. The temperature in the shade was a little cooler and every once in a while a breeze would stir to help cool her off. After about five minutes, Ollie returned with what they needed. Rachel met him at the rear of the pickup. First he tied one end of the rope to the post. Then, letting the tailgate of the pickup down, he climbed onto the bed of the truck and tied the other end to a hook made inside the bed shell. Staying inside the truck bed Ollie leaned over and pulled the tailgate shut. Looking at Rachel he said, "You can drive the truck and I'm gonna help pull from here."

"Okay, just tell me when you are ready," she replied.

As Rachel and Ollie worked, they were not aware that an audience had gathered to watch. Sherry had returned over an hour ago from the trip to Evergreen with her mother. She had been home a short time when Oscar came calling. Thinking that Dora could use a break from Molly they decided to take her for a walk. Now, standing under the oak tree that Rachel had vacated a few minutes before, they watched with interest. Realizing what they were attempting Oscar looked at Sherry and said, "That isn't going to work."

Looking up at him Sherry asked why not.

"Just watch," he said smiling.

When Ollie was set he motioned for Rachel to start. Standing in the bed of the pickup and leaning on the tailgate, Ollie held onto the rope with both hands. Rachel sat in the pickup and tried to remember where first gear was. It had been years since she had driven a standard vehicle of any kind. Thinking she had it right she put the truck in gear, and as she released the clutch she stomped on the gas harder than she intended. Inadvertently Rachel had put the truck in second gear instead of first. As she stomped on the gas the truck lurched forward and took off faster than she meant for it too. No matter how Ollie had his feet planted, he was not prepared for what happened as the truck jerked forward. When Rachel hit the gas, Ollie fell hard against the tailgate, causing it to fall open. Unable to catch himself, Ollie fell face first half way out of the truck, his foot becoming tangled in the rope. The short rope drew tight, and from the speed and strength of the pickup snapped off at the post. The recoil of the rope barely missed Ollie's head. With his hands Ollie tried to keep his face off the ground but with every bump the truck hit his face slammed into the dirt. At the same time he was trying desperately to free his foot from the rope. Suddenly his boot slipped off his foot, now free, he landed with a thud face down in a briar patch.

Looking back in the rearview mirror Rachel could not see Ollie. Panicking, she slammed the truck to a halt.

Molly was watching from under the tree, and had not missed a thing. Pointing in the direction of the truck she yelled, "Daddy's funny!"

Trying not to laugh at Molly's outburst, Oscar said to Sherry, "I knew it; that boy ain't got backing up sense!"

Afraid that Ollie was seriously hurt, both Oscar and Sherry took off at a run with Molly following behind. Before they could reach him, Ollie stood up brushing dirt off and pulling thorns from his face and hands, cussing the whole while. Looking at Rachel as she ran to his side he yelled, "God Almighty, woman, you trying to kill me or something? Where did you learn to drive anyway?"

"I'm so sorry, Ollie, I thought I was in first gear. I guess I wasn't," she said reaching to help him brush off some of the dirt.

Stepping backwards and away from her, he said, "Don't touch me."

Oscar and Sherry were close enough by this time to hear the exchange between Ollie and Rachel.

With hurt feelings showing on her face, Oscar tried to take up for her by saying, "Boy, you should have known better than to try to pull that old post up like that. Those things go so deep in the ground the only way to get them up is to dig them up!"

As hurt as her feelings were, Rachel was not about to let Ollie take the blame for what happened. Getting in Oscar's face she yelled at him, "It wasn't Ollie's idea to do it this way, it was mine!" Throwing her arms in the air Rachel again said, "I'm sorry Ollie, I didn't mean to get you hurt." Tears threatening to fall any second, Rachel ran toward the house.

Not knowing what to think by Rachel's behavior, Oscar just stood there. Sherry gently placed her hand on Ollie's arm and said, "Come on up to the house and let's see if we can get some of those stickers out of you."

Embarrassed by everything that had happened, Ollie said, "Yes ma'am."

Her hand sliding into his Molly looked up at her Daddy with sad eyes and asked, "Daddy got a boo-boo?"

Picking her up to comfort her Ollie smiled and said, "Yeah, Daddy got a boo-boo. But it doesn't hurt—see, no blood."

Seeing that Ollie wasn't bleeding, Molly smiled and said, "Daddy you funny." Wiping dirt off with her small hand she placed a kiss on his cheek.

*   *   *   *   *

Dora and Sherry had taken care of Ollie's scrapes and pulled all the thorns out that they could. Not used to being fussed over, Ollie stood it as long as he could, finally jumping up from the kitchen table and saying, "I need to get back to work. It's gonna take the rest of the day to dig that post up." Stopping at the door he turned back to the women and said, "Tell Ms. Rachel I know it was an accident. I didn't mean to yell at her." Nodding his thanks to them he left. Just as Ollie was going outside, Oscar came inside.

Realizing that Oscar had not followed them into the house, Sherry asked him where he had been. Taking a seat at the kitchen table he replied, "Needed to take a walk. I went down to the chicken house to check on Juan and Maria. Everything is all right down there."

Relieved that no other mishaps had occurred, Sherry sat down beside him and took his hand in hers. "Thank you. With everything that's happened I suppose we should keep a closer watch down there." In an effort to lighten his mood, Sherry asked him to join them for lunch.

"Thanks, but I probably shouldn't. I don't want to wear out my welcome."

Walking into the kitchen as Oscar was speaking Barbara interjected. "Nonsense, you're always welcome here. Dora, Mr. Newcume will be joining us for lunch." Oscar agreed to stay seeing he had no way of gracefully declining.

Humiliated and upset, Rachel was in a foul mood the rest of the day. Not hungry, she stayed in the parlor as everyone else ate lunch in the dining room. Standing at the window she could see Ollie diligently working at digging up the old post. Mentally recapping everything that had happened in the last several weeks, Rachel wondered if she had made the right decision to stay at the farm. Lost in her thoughts, she did not hear a car pulling up in the driveway. The knock at the door almost scared her out of her wits. Hoping it was Jake, she dashed out of the parlor and opened the front door. Disappointment flashed across her face as she stared at Alec Jamison.

Standing with his hat in his hand he smiled broadly at her and said, "Afternoon, Ms. Rachel. I hope I haven't come at a bad time."

Recovering from her disappointment quickly, she replied, "No, you haven't Alec. Won't you come in?" Stepping back and opening the door wider she let him in. Leading him into the parlor she asked, "What brings you by today?"

"I was in the area and thought I would check to see how you were recovering."

"I'm fine now. Not many headaches." Motioning for him to sit down on the couch, Rachel sat across from him on the love seat.

He placed his hat on the couch beside him, leaned back and said, "That's good to hear." Pausing he looked around the room. Not thinking of anything to say Rachel sat quietly and waited for him to say something. Alec cleared his throat and asked how business was going.

Thankful for a safe subject, Rachel responded, "Things are going okay. Ollie called and got the chickens replaced about a week ago. We shouldn't be behind in production much longer."

"That's good; so I guess you won't be needing to cut back on the amount of feed for next month," he replied.

"No, we'll keep everything the same."

Before he could make another comment, they were interrupted by voices approaching the parlor. Alec stood up when Sherry, Barbara and Oscar came into the room, and waited for Rachel to make introductions. "Alec Jamison, this is my mother, Sherry Collier, my grandmother, Mrs. Parker." Turning toward Oscar, Rachel continued, "You may already know Mr. Newcume."

Alec took each lady's hand in turn and said he was pleased to meet them, shook hands with Oscar, and said, "Yes, I know Oscar. How are you today?"

"Doing all right. Yourself?"

"Fine, thanks."

Oscar and Sherry joined Alec on the couch and Barbara sat beside Rachel on the love seat. In no time the two men started talking business, excluding the women in the room. Always hating to be left out of a conversation, Barbara interrupted the men, attempting to change the subject. "Rachel, honey, Oscar has invited us to a barbecue at his place tomorrow. Doesn't that sound like fun?"

Not really interested but not wanting to make her grandmother mad with her, Rachel agreed.

Oscar took the hint to change the subject and asked Alec to join them at the barbecue.

Making no effort to conceal his excitement over the prospect of spending more time with Rachel, Alec asked, "Are you having barbecued venison?"

"Of course, along with the usual: steaks, hamburgers and such."

"Then I'll be there. About what time?"

"We should be starting around noon. You know how these things go—we'll be cooking most of the afternoon."

Feeling a migraine coming on, Rachel stood up; following suit, both men did the same. "Please excuse me—I suddenly feel a headache coming on. I think I need to lie down for a while." Trying hard not to be rude she thanked Alec for coming and said she would see him tomorrow at Oscar's. Hurriedly she rushed from the room. She climbed the stairs two at a time and ran into her bathroom in time to throw up. This was the worst headache she'd had since getting out of the hospital. Chalking it up to too much excitement in one day, she rinsed out her mouth, wet a washcloth with cold water, then slowly walked to the bed and placed it on her forehead. She was asleep almost as soon as she closed her eyes.

CHAPTER SEVEN

Falling asleep was the best thing Rachel could have done for her migraine. Awakening in a dark room she knew it was late. Turning her head slowly she looked at the digital clock to see what time it was. The red light, glowing in the dark, said ten minutes after midnight. Her stomach growling, she realized she had missed both lunch and dinner. Easing her body into an upright position she gradually stood up. Sometimes after a headache as bad as the one she had suffered today she was dizzy when she first got up. Finding that her equilibrium was stable was a good sign. Still dressed in the clothes from the day before, she left her room and headed to the kitchen in her bare socks. The house was on the chilly side tonight, so she was thankful she had her socks on. Going into the kitchen as quietly as possible, hoping not to wake Dora, she opened the refrigerator and started to plunder. To her surprise a plate of food wrapped in plastic was sitting on the top shelf with a note addressed to her attached to it. Taking the plate from the refrigerator she pulled the note off and read it. It said:

Rachel,
Thought you might be hungry when you got up so I left this plate for you.
Dora.
P.S. Wash the plate when you're done.

Laughing softly, Rachel thought again about the change in Dora since arriving at the farm. She would have never left food prepared for her midnight raids before. Removing the plastic wrap Rachel found slices of roast beef, mashed potatoes with gravy and butter beans. After heating the plate in the microwave she decided to eat in the study.

Reaching the study doors she found them closed. Rachel set the plate on a small table in the foyer and slid one of the panel doors open. The room was dark except for a glow coming from the computer. Thinking that the alien study program must be running she retrieved her plate and went into the study. The room was colder than the kitchen had been, so she lit the logs already laid out in the fireplace. Curling up with her feet under her she quickly consumed the food on her plate. When she had finished she set the plate aside, pulled an afghan across her legs and sat staring at the flames. Soon the room was warm and cozy, and the hum of the computer and the warmth of the fire lulled Rachel back to sleep.

Dreaming peacefully of Jake, she felt his hand on her face. Suddenly a cold chill came over her and she jerked awake. Laughing at herself she tried to tell herself it was only a dream. No one had really been in the room and touched her face; fright from all of the unexplained events was making her imagination run wild. Looking around the room she could tell she had been asleep for some time because the fire had died down. That would also explain why she was chilled.

The only sound in the room was the occasional snap of the last log still burning, and she noticed the computer was no longer running. Thinking it must have shut itself off, she stood up and closed the grill over the fireplace to make the fire die on out. Remembering Dora's message she picked up her plate and started for the kitchen. Stepping into the foyer she glanced at the front door to be sure it was locked; it wasn't. Trying desperately not to panic she reached for the door to turn the lock when suddenly the doorknob started turning. Fear racing through her veins, Rachel looked for something to use as a weapon. Finding nothing, she stepped back into the study and quietly slid the door almost shut. Getting on her knees she peeked out the crack she had left between the doors and watched to see what the intruder was up to.

Barbara slowly closed the front door as she came inside. Dressed in her floor length robe and slippers, she carefully re-locked the front door. As she turned around, Rachel saw her grandmother place a pack of cigarettes in the pocket of her robe. Stepping lightly in her slippers, Barbara climbed the stairs and entered her bedroom.

First relief took the place of the fear in Rachel's veins, then humor. The episode really wasn't funny, but Rachel now had a secret on her grandmother. For the last several weeks Sherry and Dora had been monitoring the number of cigarettes Barbara smoked. They thought she was down to half a pack a day and were trying to cut it down even more. Retracing her footsteps to the kitchen, Rachel decided she would keep her grandmother's secret for a little while. Her plate washed and dried, Rachel went back upstairs and crawled back into bed.

* * * * *

When Rachel woke the next morning, the first thing she noticed was the smell of cinnamon and spices. Wondering what delicious concoctions

Dora had going in the kitchen, she hurried through her morning routine and went down the back stairs. Coming into the kitchen Rachel saw two pecan pies cooling on the counter top. She knew this was not where the cinnamon smell was coming from, so she stepped to the oven to take a peek inside. Just before she opened the oven door, Dora came out of the pantry and said, "If you make my pies fall, Ms. Rachel, I'll have your head."

Putting both hands behind her back just like a little kid caught doing something they knew was wrong, she asked, "What kind of pies, Dora?"

"I found some sweet potatoes down in the root cellar yesterday; thought I would use them before they went bad."

"Ummm." Pecan and sweet potato pies were Rachel's favorite. She was going to have to have a piece of both. Going back to the counter she pointed at the pecan pies and asked, "Are these cool enough to cut?"

"No, and we aren't eating them. I'm sending them with you to the barbecue at Mr. Oscar's today."

Disappointed, Rachel said, "Oh." She had forgotten all about the barbecue. Sighing she asked, "Where is everyone this morning?"

"Your grandmother is in the parlor. Ms. Sherry left about an hour ago—said Mr. Oscar invited her over early so they could go horseback riding before everyone arrived."

Seeing the look on Rachel's face, Dora continued, "And you can just get over it. It's about time Ms. Sherry started thinking about herself and found a man she can spend time with." Not saying anything more Dora went back to her cooking.

Rachel thought about what Dora had said as she went down the hall toward the parlor. She found Barbara sitting on the couch reading, with her feet propped up on a tapestry covered ottoman. Sitting down across from her grandmother, Rachel said, "Grandmother, I'm worried about Mother."

Setting her book aside, Barbara looked at Rachel and said, "Why?"

"Well, it's just that she has never...well—"

"Spit it out child!"

"I'm not sure if I like her spending so much time with Mr. Newcume. I mean, what do we really know about him?"

"Is that all? Well I think Oscar is a fine gentleman, the kind of man your mother should have found a long time ago. If it makes you feel any better I'll tell you what my investigator found out about him."

Shocked Rachel exclaimed, "Grandmother! You didn't have him checked out, did you?"

"Of course I did. I always do on anyone your mother or you show an interest in. You both stand to inherit a good amount of money when I leave this earth, and I have to make sure you aren't going to be swindled out of it!"

"You mean you had Jason checked out?"

Nodding her head yes, Barbara asked, "Well, do you want to know about Oscar or not?"

Mortified that her grandmother would do such a thing, she said no and left the room. Passing the grandfather clock in the hall she glanced to see what time it was. Thinking she had time before she would have to dress for the barbecue she decided to take a walk.

* * * * *

Following the directions left by her mother, Rachel and her grandmother drove to the barbecue. Because she had skipped breakfast that morning the aromas emanating from the back seat were making Rachel hungry. As promised, Dora had sent two pecan pies and two sweet potato pies along with a batch of her fabulous chocolate chip cookies. As she drove Rachel wondered who would be there. She hoped Jake would take time out of his day to stop by. She still had not seen him since she'd gotten out of the hospital.

The drive to Oscars' place was not very far. They traveled south about half a mile on Highway

31, and turned right onto Highway 26 heading west. Four miles down Highway 26, Rachel turned off the paved road and onto a private dirt lane. She realized that Oscars' house was the original plantation home that her farmhouse had once been part of. The lane was only big enough for one vehicle to pass through at a time, and she prayed she didn't meet anyone coming out or one of them would have to back up. Huge old oak trees formed a canopy over the lane on both sides, and a forest of pines grew thick behind the oaks. The effect was almost claustrophobic. After driving for about a mile the lane suddenly opened into a vast lawn and a beautiful view of the house was exposed. The old plantation had partially burned in the early 1900's, but now it was restored to its full glory. Sitting on a slope, from the front the house looked like it was only two stories high. A porch ran the entire length of the front of the house with four large white columns supporting the top of it. The left side of the lawn was being used as a parking lot. By the number of vehicles already there, Rachel could tell this would be a large party. Her grandmother helping her carry the box of desserts, they followed the stream of people to the back side of the house. From there Rachel saw that the house really had three stories instead of two. A deck ran the length of the middle floor, and underneath it was a beautiful sunroom.

Finally locating her mother they started in her direction. When they reached her, Sherry showed them where to put the box of goodies. This was not a catered affair, but more of an old-fashioned dinner on the ground gathering. Long tables were set up on the back lawn for the food. Behind them several large barbecue grills were all going at once with several men stepping up to assist with the cooking of the varied meats. Lawn chairs of all kinds were spread out across the lawn, some under oak trees to be out of the sun while others, men mostly, were sitting in lawn chairs down by a pond, fishing. Behind the grills a covered concrete area was set up with musical instruments. A musical system of some sort was playing now, but Rachel thought at some point they must be having live entertainment.

"Where is Oscar?" Barbara asked.

"He's over at the barbecue grills supervising the cooking," replied Sherry.

Taking Barbara by the hand Sherry said, "Come on, Mother, and I'll get you something to drink. Then I want to reintroduce you to an old friend of yours."

On her own, Rachel looked around at the crowd hoping to see someone she knew. Scanning a group at the tables, she saw Roxanne and waved at her. Walking in that direction, Roxanne and another woman met her half way. The other woman was very statuesque and looked like a model. The woman's long dark hair full of natural curls flowed freely down her back. Rachel could honestly say she was one of the most beautiful women she had ever seen.

"It's about time you got here—I was beginning to think you weren't coming," said Roxanne. "Rachel, this is Christi Reynolds."

Recognizing the name, Rachel smiled and said, "It's nice to meet you, Christi. I was in your boutique the other day. I loved your designs!"

Laughing, Christi responded, "I guess you did; that one you have on looks good on you."

Rachel had not known what to wear to this affair, so she had chosen something safe and worn the pink skirt and blouse she had bought at the boutique. "Thank you, I do like it, but now that I've met you, I must say I'm surprised that you make petite clothes."

Not offended by the comment Christi replied, "I have a teenage daughter who models for my petite designs; although as fast as she is growing, I may not be able to use her much longer. You wouldn't be interested in the job would you?"

Flattered by the question, Rachel remarked, "Maybe. It sounds like fun."

Before the ladies could continue their conversation they were interrupted by a voice from behind. Turning to see who was addressing them, Rachel looked straight into Alec's eyes. Startled by the intensity in them she said, "Hello, Alec. Do you know Roxanne Hinton and Christi Reynolds?"

"I've met them; how are you ladies today? Fine weather for a barbecue, isn't it?"

Roxanne found her voice first, responding, "Yes, it is. Oops, I see Ollie left Molly unattended again. I better go get her before she wanders down to the pond and falls in!"

"I'll help you," was all Christi could think of to say as the two of them left Rachel alone with Alec.

Alec had been standing there holding a glass of champagne in each hand. Handing one to Rachel, jokingly he asked, "Was it something I said?

Laughing Rachel said, "I don't think so."

"I'm glad you came. Are you feeling better today? I mean you looked kind of pale yesterday when you left so abruptly."

Smiling brightly, Rachel answered, "Yes I feel much better today. Thanks for asking." As they talked they began walking around the yard. Reaching the side of the house they stopped at the side of a formal flower garden. A vine covered gazebo stood in the middle of the garden. Half way to the gazebo they heard voices behind them, and turned around to see who was coming. Standing there was Jake with a woman Rachel had not met.

Shaking hands with Alec, Jake introduced the woman who was hanging onto his arm. "Bonnie Banks, I would like you to meet Rachel Collier and Alec Jamison."

Jealousy cruised through Rachel's whole body, making her bite her tongue. Keeping her catty remark to herself, she observed that Bonnie was attractive but not a raving beauty. She was average height, about two inches taller than Rachel, with shoulder length auburn hair. By her porcelain skin Rachel could tell Bonnie never spent much time in the sun. Bonnie's hair and crystal, blue eyes were the only thing that kept her from looking like a ghost.

When she spoke her heavy southern accent made Rachel wonder if it was phony. Smiling sweetly Bonnie addressed both Rachel and Alec saying, "It's so nice to meet you both. Are you from around here?"

Before either of them could answer, Jake responded to her question. "Rachel is Darlyn MacKinstry's niece, and Alec owns Jamison Feed Company over in Andalusia."

Her eyes growing wide with the prospect of some juicy gossip, Bonnie said, "Oh, dear, I'm so sorry to hear about your aunt. She was always such a kind person. It was a shame about her accident. Are you going to be taking over the farm now that she is gone? I mean the house is nice and all, but that smell! How do you put up with it?"

Cutting into Bonnie's bombardment of questions, Jake spoke up saying, "Alec, would you do me a favor and take Bonnie for a drink? She was telling me she was thirsty before we ran into the two of you. I need to speak to Rachel alone for a few minutes. Police business, you understand." As he was talking he finally managed to pry Bonnie's hand off his arm and place it on Alec's.

Looking at Rachel, Alec caught a glimmer of something in her eyes. He wasn't sure if it was anger, jealousy, or hope. "Would you like me to bring you anything Rachel?" he asked. Her eyes never leaving Jake's, she said no thanks.

Jake took Rachel by the elbow and guided her away from the other couple before Bonnie could ask any more questions. He had been trying to get away from her for the last half hour. Stepping into the vine covered gazebo they were finally alone. Without saying a word Jake pulled Rachel into his arms and kissed her. Startled at first, she tried to pull away but the feel of his lips crushing hers made a fire start to burn deep inside. Wrapping her arms around his neck she kissed him back with everything she felt.

Slowly releasing her he stepped back, but still kept his hands on her arms. Gently rubbing her forearms with his hands he said, "Thank you ma'am, for rescuing me from Bonnie. That woman latches on to me every chance she gets." Sighing he continued, "But I'm not about to be the fourth bee in her bonnet." Rachel gave Jake a puzzled look, so he added, "Ask Roxanne about her sometime. I don't want to talk about her right now." Starting to pull Rachel back toward him, she put her hands on his chest and stopped him from kissing her again.

"I thought you wanted to talk police business," she said.

"I do, but you are making it hard for me to keep my mind on work."

Stepping out of his arms, she smiled and said, "This should make it easier. Now tell me, have you found anything that might help catch the person who attacked me?"

"Unfortunately no. But, the day of the attack you left a message for me to call you. I was hoping you had something that might help."

Remembering her visit into Evergreen and the sheriff's office, Rachel exclaimed, "Oh, I'd forgotten all about it." Laughing she said, "It's nothing, I think I know what happened. It's not important now."

It was Jake's turn to look puzzled and he said, "Maybe you should start at the beginning and tell me what had you so worked up. I'll decide if it's important or not."

Embarrassed at causing him so much trouble, she persisted, "Really, it's nothing."

"Tell me!" he said clinching his jaw in frustration.

"Oh all right, but don't you laugh when I tell you!"

Jake took a deep breath, trying to stay calm, and said, "Okay."

"The night before I came to your office I thought someone had broken into the house."

"What! And you're just now telling—"

"No one broke in, so just calm down and listen!" she interrupted before he got too upset. Although he paced the floor of the gazebo as he listened, he didn't interrupt. She told him everything, beginning with the noise that woke them to finding the door open. Saying that, she shot him a look that said not to talk, so he stood still and listened to the rest of her explanation. When she told him about Darlyn's alien project on the computer and seeing her grandmother sneaking into the house after a smoke, Jake started to laugh.

"You said you wouldn't laugh!" she pouted.

"I'm sorry," he apologized and took her into his arms again. "You've been through so much in the last couple of weeks, I'm sure it's not funny to you." Kissing her lightly on the nose he asked, "Will you have dinner with me tomorrow night?"

Smiling warmly she said, "I don't know, can you cook?"

"I'm a bachelor; it was either learn to cook or starve," he chuckled.

"Good, because I can't cook a thing!" she laughed. "What time?"

"Is eight o'clock okay?"

"Eight is fine. I'll be there."

"I'll call you tomorrow and give you directions."

A loud noise at the entrance of the gazebo startled both of them. Turning in that direction, Jake saw his Uncle Russell and Oscar standing there.

"There you are Jake, we've been looking all over for you," said his uncle. Nodding at Rachel, he asked, "You gonna introduce your uncle to this pretty young lady, or do I need to do it myself?"

Taking Rachel by the hand, Jake introduced his uncle to Rachel. "It's nice to meet you, Mr. Brewer," she said.

"Call me Russ, everybody does. It's nice to meet you too. I've known your Aunt Darlyn for many years. She's a hard act to follow, if you know what I mean," he commented. Rachel wasn't sure what he meant by that so she did the polite thing and kept her mouth shut.

Frustrated by the interruption Jake asked, "Uncle Russell, did you and Oscar need me for something?"

Oscar spoke up for the first time, answering Jake's question, "Yes, Jake we do need to speak to you privately. I'm sure Rachel will give us a few minutes alone, won't you my dear?"

"There's plenty of food out there, why don't you go fix yourself a plate and we'll send this fellow on his way when we're finished talking," added Russell.

Feeling like a child being told to get lost by a couple of bullies, Rachel responded as gracefully as she could, "Take your time gentlemen; I'm sure whatever you have to discuss with Jake is important." Holding her head high as she left the gazebo, she wondered if they needed to discuss her aunt's death. Rachel knew that Russell had been the former sheriff, but she couldn't understand why

Oscar would need to be in on the discussion if that was what it was about. Standing outside the gazebo, Rachel admired the flower garden. Without realizing it she had wandered closer to the side of the gazebo. Stooping to smell the yellow roses just starting to bloom, she overheard something that made her freeze.

"My sources tell me that several local farms have gone bust the last few years. I'm not sure why, but rumor has it that they were run out of business one way or another."

"You suspect foul play?" Recognizing Jake's voice she knew he had asked this question.

"My sources will only say so much. But, Oscar here has done some investigating for me on the financial end and it looks like the same company has bought all the farms. You tell him what you told me, Oscar," said Russell.

"It's a dummy corporation is all I know at this time. I don't know who the primary stockholder is or what they plan on doing with the property. I'm still looking into it."

Hearing this conversation, Rachel realized that the reason her aunt had been killed was because some stranger wanted her property. Feeling ill and angry, she started toward the house. As she entered the sunroom, she saw several older ladies sitting and reminiscing about other parties in the area. Her grandmother sat among them acting as if she was enjoying herself. Slipping through the room without her grandmother seeing her, Rachel headed down a hallway hoping to find a bathroom. Still feeling ill from what she had heard, she thought she would feel better if she washed her face. The end of this hallway crossed with another and as she neared the other hallway she could hear voices talking very low. Not sure who she would be encountering she ducked behind a large potted plant in the corner, waiting for them to pass. She could not see the two people, but she could tell it was two men having a heated argument. From where she was she could only hear pieces of their conversation. Hearing MacKinstry Farm mentioned by one of the men, Rachel's ears strained to hear more.

"I'm telling you boss, I can't get near that place right now. The sheriff's got patrols night and day. Now they even got a couple of Mexican's working for them. Those two are there all day; won't even leave for lunch anymore."

"That's your fault for doing a half ass job with that Collier girl. You've got them all worked up. We'll just have to wait awhile and try again later. But I will get my hands on that farm! Now get out of here, before someone sees you talking to me!"

Hearing the two men walk away in opposite directions, Rachel slowly released the breath from her lungs. She hadn't realized she had been holding her breath until she let it out. Really feeling ill now, Rachel stepped out from behind the plant and started to turn the corner. When she did she ran into Molly with Roxanne following close behind.

Molly was holding the cutest little dog. Stopping her, Rachel asked, "Where did you find that pretty little dog, Molly?"

Holding it closer she said with tears in her eyes, "It's my doggie!"

Finally catching up to her niece, Roxanne bent down and said, "Molly, sweetheart, you know that Toodle belongs to Mr. Oscar. He said you could play with her while you are here, but you will have to leave her with him when we go home."

Stomping her tiny foot she insisted that Toodle was her dog, and turning the corner, ran in the direction of the sunroom.

Roxanne looked at Rachel and said, "Kids, what do you do with them?" Seeing how peeked Rachel looked she asked, "Are you all right, honey?"

"Yea...yes, I'm just looking for the bathroom. Do you know where it is?"

"You're standing in front of it."

Not wanting to get into a lengthy discussion with Roxanne, Rachel said, "Thanks; you might better go after Molly, before she stashes that little dog in your car."

"She probably will if she thinks of it. See you later," she said as she followed in Molly's wake.

Turning around, Rachel found the bathroom door behind her just as Roxanne had said it was. Knocking to be sure it was not occupied she closed the door behind her and locked it. Leaning against the door, it came to her that Roxanne might have passed one of the two men in the hallway. She was going to have to get herself together and go look for Roxanne. Going to the sink, she splashed cold water on her face and tried to start thinking logically. Remembering the conversation, she thought she might have recognized one of the voices but she couldn't place it. Leaving the bathroom feeling a little better, Rachel started back to the sunroom. Going to her grandmother's side she asked, "Grandmother, did you eat yet? Would you like me to go fix you a plate?"

Smiling proudly at her granddaughter, Barbara said, "Yes, Rachel, I've eaten. Honey, you don't know this lady sitting next to me, but AnneMerle and I were best friends when I lived here. We've been catching up on all the gossip."

"It's nice to meet you, ma'am. I'll let you two get back to your gossiping," she giggled, and after kissing her grandmother on the cheek she headed out the door.

Rachel spent the rest of the afternoon wandering around from group to group. Finally speaking to a friendly group of ladies, Rachel asked if they had seen Roxanne. Laughing all at once, one of the women said, "Yea, we saw her. She came flying out of the house chasing after that wild little niece of hers. Molly was chasing Oscar's dog. I got to admit that little dog is pretty smart! It headed straight for the pond, and just at the last second it made a U-turn. Poor Molly slid right into the pond...Roxanne had to go in after her! Caused such a commotion, I'm surprised you missed it!" Giggling again, she told Rachel that Roxanne took Molly home. Thanking her, Rachel went to get something to eat.

By the time the live music started her head was spinning. She had seen Jake only one other time that afternoon. He told her he couldn't stay any longer because he needed to get back to work. Reminding her that he would call her tomorrow, he had kissed her briefly and left. Spotting her mother sitting in one of the lawn chairs, she joined her. The music was mostly local people taking turns singing or playing. Some were pretty good while others were not so good. The melodies ranged from old country classics to modern country with a little gospel thrown in. After about an hour Rachel stood up, stretching, and said, "I think I'll see if Grandmother is ready to go home; I'm exhausted. Do you have a way home?"

Not sure how her daughter was going to react, Sherry said, "Oscar has asked me to spend the night. I think I'm going to."

Rachel didn't like the idea, but she wasn't up to an argument with her mother. Saying good night she headed back to the house. Barbara was just coming outside when Rachel reached the door. "There you are—I wasn't sure if you were still inside or not. Are you ready to go home?" Rachel asked.

Making a funny face at the sound of the music, Barbara said, "Well, I don't want to stay and listen to any of that racket. If you are ready to leave, let's go."

Darkness was rapidly falling as Rachel and Barbara reached the farm. Parking the car in front of the house they both went inside. Dora met them in the foyer. "How was the barbecue?" she asked.

"Fine, Dora, I got caught up on all the gossip that's happened since we've been gone. I'll tell you everything tomorrow," said Barbara. "I'm tired and going to bed. See you both in the morning." Kissing Rachel good night, Barbara started up the stairs.

"Can I get you anything, Ms. Rachel?" Dora asked.

"No thanks, Dora, I'm stuffed. By the way, your pies were a big success. I think they were the first things gone on the dessert table."

Proudly, Dora nodded and said, "Good. Well if you don't need anything I guess I'll retire to my room. Good night, Ms. Rachel."

"Good night, Dora." Watching Dora walk down the hallway, Rachel again wondered why Dora was being so friendly lately. Shrugging off the thought Rachel turned and double-checked the front door to be sure it was locked and went upstairs to her room. Checking the time, Rachel decided it was not too late to call Roxanne.

After four rings the phone was answered on the other end. "Hello, Roxanne? This is Rachel. I'm sorry to call you so late but I need to ask you a question."

"Oh hey, Rachel, what's up?"

"Well, I just wanted to know if you remembered when we ran into each other in the house at Oscar's this afternoon, did you pass anyone in the hall before you saw me?"

Wondering what this was about, Roxanne asked, "No, not a soul. Why?"

Her story all ready, Rachel said, "Oh, I just overheard a man talking and I thought it was

someone I used to know…you know, when I used to spend the summers with Aunt Darlyn. I just can't remember who he is, that's all."

"Well, sorry I couldn't help you. Listen, honey I got to go put Molly to bed. I'll talk to you later." Before Rachel could say anything else the line went dead. Hanging up the phone, Rachel got ready for bed.

Susan Weekley

CHAPTER EIGHT

As the final guest drove away, Oscar put his arm around Sherry's shoulder and walked her inside the house. Stepping into the sunken den he asked her if she would like a glass of wine. Fighting a last minute morality attack, she said yes, hoping it would calm her nerves. What Sherry didn't realize was that Oscar was having the same feelings. Pouring them both a glass of Merlot he handed one to her and guided her to the couch.

Sherry was trying to think of something witty to say when Toodle bounced into her lap. Laughing she said, "God, I wish I had this much energy. I think she enjoyed the barbecue as much as everyone else. Did you see what happened to Roxanne?"

Grinning at the sound of Sherry's laughter, Oscar replied, "Yea, I saw what happened to Roxanne and her niece." Reaching over and patting the dog on the head he continued, "I should have named you Mischief, the way you are always into trouble."

"Where did you come up with the name Toodle anyway? I mean, it is kind of unusual."

"The man I bought her from told me she was a toy poodle, so I named her Toodle. It seemed to fit the little ball of fur. It wasn't until she got a little bigger that I realized she isn't a toy poodle. I had to do some research on dogs, but I finally found a picture of a dog on the Internet that looked just like her. She is really a Maltese."

At that moment as if on cue, Toodle jumped out of Sherry's lap and pranced out of the room. "There she goes again; what do you think she's up to?" asked Sherry.

"Anything; she is probably looking for her favorite sock to play with." Changing the subject Oscar asked, "Did you really have a good time today?"

Smiling sincerely at Oscar, she answered, "It was a nice barbecue. I've really enjoyed the day."

"I did too, but there is something I've been wanting to do all day." Saying that, Oscar leaned forward and kissed her. The feel of his lips on hers made her shiver so hard she almost dropped the glass of wine. It had been a long time since Sherry had been kissed with so much passion. Her blood pumping, she kissed Oscar back. Coming up for air, Oscar took her glass and placed it on the coffee table. Before she knew what was happening Oscar was kissing her again. But as he kissed her he picked her up and carried her upstairs. By the time they reached the top of the stairs their passion was in full bloom. Pushing a door open with his foot, Oscar carried Sherry into the bedroom.

They made love the first time like teenagers, only better. At their age they learned quickly how to please each other. Exhausted, they lay in each other's arms and talked.

"I haven't made love with a woman since my wife died. Haven't wanted to," said Oscar. "There's just something about you, Sherry, that makes me feel young again. I don't exactly know how to explain it."

Sherry pulled him closer, and said, "You don't have to, I know what you're talking about." Kissing him on the chest she smiled up into his face. "You make me feel young again too. Maybe too young," she giggled.

Lifting an eyebrow he asked, "Why do you say that?"

Sliding upward she whispered in Oscar's ear.

"Oh you do? Well now, little lady, I think we can handle that." Rolling her over on her back he began to make love to her again. Sometime after midnight the two fell asleep tangled in a lover's embrace.

*   *   *   *   *

Rachel tried to stay busy the next day. Her anticipation of the evening alone with Jake grew with each passing hour. The conversation she had overheard between Jake and his uncle made her worry, so she spent most of the morning in the study going over the farm's accounts. Reassured that the farm was in no financial danger she felt a little better until she thought about the other conversation she had overheard. She definitely would have to tell Jake about it tonight. Knowing the person responsible for her attack had been at the barbecue made her paranoid. Was it someone she had met only yesterday, or was it someone she already knew? The one thing she was sure of was that it was a man.

Rachel heard the front door open and went to see who it was. She met Sherry and Oscar in the foyer, and after kissing her mother good morning, she asked, "Did you enjoy yourself last night?" Seeing both Sherry and Oscar blush she quickly added, "At the barbecue I mean."

Laughing Sherry said, "Yes, we did. Did you have a good time? I saw you talking to Alec. He seems like a nice young man."

Continuing their conversation in the parlor, Rachel answered Sherry's question. "I only talked to him for a few minutes, then I didn't see him for the rest of the afternoon. He may have left early, but there were so many people there I can't be sure." Thinking this was the perfect opportunity she looked at Oscar and asked, "How many people were there do you think? I mean, did you have an invitation list?"

"This is the country, Rachel, you don't send out formal invitations. People hear about it by word of mouth. You never know who's going to show up. But you can always count on good food and a lot of people!"

Trying to hide the disappointment she felt, she said, "Oh, I see." Changing the subject she asked, "So what have you two been up to this morning?"

The look that passed between Sherry and Oscar was startling to Rachel. If she didn't know better she would think they looked like lovebirds. Not wanting a mental picture of that she tried to dismiss it from her mind. Sherry rescued her from her thoughts by saying, "We went horseback riding again this morning. Oscar has some beautiful horses in his stable."

"I don't recall seeing a stable yesterday," said Rachel.

"Oh, it's not at the house. You have to drive further down the lane to reach it. I don't get much time to spend with the horses like I used too. My foreman lives over the stable in an apartment and he takes care of them. Between the actual working of the fields and my other financial responsibilities I stay too busy. You can't see the fields from the house either. I'm not bragging now, but my place is so big that the rest of my workers live in several duplex apartments I built about a year ago. Now days we have whole families who come in to help work the fields. It's not like the old days where a bunkhouse held men only. That's where Maria and Juan stay when they leave here every day."

"Oh, I didn't realize your farm was that big. Were some of your workers at the barbecue yesterday?" Rachel asked, thinking that maybe one of the men she had overheard was one of Oscar's workers.

"Of course. I always include my workers in all the activities. It's part of their benefits, I guess you could say."

"I see," said Rachel. A lull in the conversation made Rachel start to fidget. Finally she said, "Well, speaking of workers, I think I'll go down to the chicken house and see how things are going." Saying good-bye to Oscar she left the house.

When she entered the main room she found Ollie, Juan and Maria all sitting on the couch eating lunch. Remembering that it was lunchtime, she told them she would come back later and give them a hand. Inviting her to stay saying they had plenty, they shared their lunch with her. After lunch Rachel sat down at a workstation and started cleaning eggs. This time she was not alone—Maria was with her all afternoon. Although Rachel was enjoying Maria's company, she noticed Maria never left her side for a minute. When Maria followed her into the refrigeration room to store the clean eggs, Rachel said, "Maria, don't take this wrong, but I get the feeling you don't want me left alone. Either that or you don't think I know what I'm doing."

"Oh, I know you know what you're doing, Ms. Rachel. I'm sorry if I've made you feel uncomfortable. I'm just doing what the sheriff told us to do."

"Jake? What did he tell you to do, Maria?"

"He said anytime you come down to the chicken house we weren't to leave you by yourself. I guess he was worried that something else might happen to you."

Rachel was secretly pleased that Jake cared enough about her to have someone looking out for her when he wasn't around. But knowing that someone was out there ready to harm her or anyone around her, she didn't feel comfortable being at the chicken house any longer. The idea of Maria or anyone else getting hurt because they were babysitting her made Rachel angry with Jake. She finished storing the eggs and said, "I have other things to take care of, so I'll let you get back to work. Talk to you later, Maria." Not saying anything else she left the chicken house and walked to the farmhouse.

The sun was getting low in the sky as Rachel left the chicken house, so engrossed in her own thoughts about her feelings for Jake and being angry with him at the same time, she didn't see the man standing at the side of the chicken house. He managed to reach the end of the building without being seen by anyone. He knew he risked being caught, coming here before it was really dark, but he knew he had to get the job done before Ollie locked up for the night. Quickly finishing the job he had come to do, he left the same way he always did.

*   *   *   *   *

By the time Rachel was ready to go to Jake's for dinner, she was a bundle of nerves. Going into the kitchen to get the bottle of wine she had thought to chill after returning from the chicken house, she jumped when her grandmother spoke behind her.

"I see you are ready for your date. Here, you might need this," she said handing her a piece of paper.

"What is it?"

"Directions to his house...I don't think you've been there before, have you?"

"No ma'am, I haven't—thanks," she said taking the paper.

Opening the refrigerator Barbara took out a plastic bowl and put it in a paper sack. Handing it to Rachel she said, "Here, take this to Jake. I told him I'd send something along to go with your dinner."

Taking the bag, Rachel kissed her grandmother and said thanks. Reading over the directions to Jake's house, she found that he lived in town. She had assumed that he lived in the country, but being sheriff she guessed it made more sense that he lived closer to his office. "I need to hurry or I'm going to be late. Don't wait up for me, I'm not sure what time I'll be home."

"You be home at a respectable hour, young lady. I'm an old woman and I don't need to be up all night worried about you!"

"Oh, Grandmother, what could possibly happen? What could be safer than spending time with the sheriff?"

"I guess you have a point," Barbara relented. "But try not to stay out too late, okay?"

"Yes, ma'am." Hugging her grandmother, Rachel left for Jake's.

Reaching the city limits, she mentally went over the directions she had read. Taking the first right after crossing the bridge into town and making another right at a stop sign, another right and then a left, Rachel ended up on a street that took her parallel with the bridge. The road curved and went downhill, but she found Jake's house with no trouble. Getting out of the car she looked at the house. In the gathering darkness, she wasn't sure if the house was in a state of restoration or ready to be condemned. The front light was burning and as she walked up the steps to the front porch she could see holes in some of the floorboards. Stepping lightly to the door, it opened before she could knock.

Smiling broadly Jake warned, "Enter at your own risk. Anything in your way, step over it or move it."

Laughing at the unusual greeting she replied, "Well, hello to you too!" Entering the house she immediately understood why he had said what he did. The house was in complete disorder. Amazed at the chaos Rachel just stood and looked around.

"A mess isn't it."

Trying to be diplomatic she said, "Let's just say it's not what I expected."

His turn to laugh, he said, "Come on back to the kitchen. It will be more to your liking I think."

Following Jake to the kitchen was tricky to say the least. She had to squeeze between a ladder and the wall, step over an assortment of tools and paint cans before she reached the kitchen. Walking into the kitchen she thought she had stepped through the looking glass. In front of her was a fully remodeled kitchen complete with new appliances. Blue tile counter tops graced white cabinets. An island workspace separated part of the kitchen from the breakfast nook. Setting her bottle of wine and the paper bag on the counter, she looked at the professional job done in the kitchen, and asked, "Did you do this yourself?"

"Yep, when I can find the time. That's why the rest of the house looks like it does; I'm taking a room at a time in order of priority. The master bedroom and bath are the only other rooms I've finished inside." Opening the French doors and leading her outside, he continued, "This is what I've done outside." Stepping out onto a newly laid deck, she looked out on the backyard.

"This is nice. You have a large backyard. It would look better with the grass cut though," she teased.

"You're welcome to come do it any time you like, smarty pants!" he teased back.

"Maybe I will, and plant some flowers while I'm at it!" she said indignantly.

Still teasing her, he put his arm around her shoulder and said, "Flowers would be nice; might make it homier. What kind did you have in mind?"

Stepping away from his arm she turned and punched him in the shoulder saying, "Hire a gardener, Sheriff. I'm not your wife."

Chuckling he said, "I was just teasing you, Rachel. Come on inside while I start getting supper ready." Seeing the wine on the counter where she had left it he asked if she would like a glass.

"I wasn't sure what we were having for dinner; I hope white wine is okay."

"I always heard white was for fish and red was for pasta. That's the end of my wine knowledge. So I guess this should do fine since I thought I would fry some catfish." Picking up the bag and looking inside, he removed the plastic bowl and placed it in the refrigerator before opening the wine. As he opened the bottle he caught her looking around the kitchen. Smiling he said, "You do like fresh catfish don't you? I caught them myself out at Uncle

Russell's fish pond." Still not getting a response from her he handed her a glass of wine saying, "Earth to Rachel!"

Snapping out of her reverie, she realized that Jake was talking to her. Embarrassed, she blushed and said thanks as she accepted the glass of wine. "And yes, I do like catfish."

Touching her cheek with his fingertips, he said, "Where did you go just then?"

Seeing the worried look on his face, she smiled up at him and said, "I was just looking at this wonderful kitchen and thinking to myself that even I might be able to learn to cook in a kitchen like this. It looks like it came out of one of those magazines that showcase beautiful homes."

"It did come out of a magazine…a home improvement one at least." Desire rising in him, he stepped back and said, "I better go start the fire for the fish or we won't be eating any time soon." Never before had just looking at a woman made Jake almost lose control, but Rachel was so beautiful all he could think about was making love to her. Telling himself to slow down or he was going to blow his plans for the evening, he went outside and started the fire under the gas cooker he had set up earlier.

When he came back inside Rachel was standing by the breakfast table. Seeing that the table was all set she turned and asked, "What can I do to help?"

Taking a clean paper bag from a drawer he said, "Nothing. I'm just going to batter these fish and fix some hushpuppies to go with what you brought. It shouldn't take too long and supper will be ready."

Curiosity finally hitting her, she asked, "What was in that bowl any way?"

"Some of Ms. Dora's coleslaw, or at least that's what your grandmother suggested when I talked to her today."

"Oh. Dora makes the best coleslaw!"

Refilling their wine as Jake battered the fish, Rachel tried to think of the best way to bring up the subject she wanted to discuss with him. As if he could read her mind he said, "Uncle Russell and Oscar had some news that might be a lead about what's happening out at your farm." Thankful that she would not have to admit to eavesdropping, she listened as he told her what she already knew. But then he told her something that she didn't know. "One other thing I learned today was that all the farms that have gone bust were owned by women."

"That's interesting, but it still doesn't help much, does it?"

Walking outside he started putting the fish in the hot oil to fry. Rachel followed him and was leaning against the rail waiting for him to answer her question. Finally he said, "I'm sure it's a clue, I just don't know how it fits into the puzzle yet. This is almost ready—will you go get the hushpuppy mix out of the refrigerator for me?"

"Sure," she replied.

As she went into the kitchen she thought how nice it was to have a man cooking for her. The entire time she had dated Jason he had never done anything this domestic.

Retrieving the hushpuppy mix she returned to the deck. "Here you go," she said handing him the bowl. Deciding now was as good a time as any, she continued, "Jake, something happened at the barbecue yesterday. I think I should tell you about it."

Tension and concern radiated off him, "What happened? When? Did Alec do something to hurt you?" Jealousy flashed in his eyes.

"Alec? No, I didn't see Alec again after you ran him off." Seeing the look on his face she was pleased to see his jealousy, but didn't say anything about it. Telling him about the conversation she overheard in the hallway, she thought he would be pleased that she had a clue that might help his investigation. Instead, he got angry. Turning off the fire under the frying pot, he stormed into the kitchen and placed the food on the table. Stunned by his reaction, Rachel followed him inside. Turning around, Jake grabbed her by the arms and said, "Do you know how stupid that was? You could have been hurt!"

Realizing too late that he was hurting her himself, he loosened his grip and apologized saying, "I'm sorry, sweetheart, I don't mean to scare you. I just don't want anything else to happen to you!" Gently pulling her into his arms, this time he kissed her softly at first, then the fire inside him made the kiss turn more passionate. Stopping himself before he lost complete control, he released her.

Not sure how she felt about what just happened, Rachel smiled and said, "Maybe we should eat, before it gets cold."

Regaining some of his composure, he agreed. Taking the coleslaw out and placing it on the table he pulled a chair out for her to sit in. As they ate, Rachel tried to think of something to say. Thinking it best if they didn't discuss the case she decided to ask him about Bonnie. "Tell me, what did you mean yesterday when you said you weren't going to be the fourth bee in Bonnie's bonnet?"

Laughing, he said, "I forgot I said that. Roxanne got me started with that. It's a little joke between us. You see Bonnie has been married three times, each time to a man whose last name starts with a "B". Since my last name is Brewer…well you get the picture."

Now it was Rachel's turn to be jealous. "Yea, I get the picture. The way she was hanging onto your arm yesterday I don't think you were discouraging her."

The last thing Jake wanted was to get into an argument and spoil the evening. Ignoring Rachel's statement he asked, "Are you finished eating? You want another glass of wine?"

Afraid she had made Jake mad, she said, "Yes, to both. Let me clean the table while you get us some more wine."

"You don't have to do that."

"It's the least I can do after the fine dinner you just fed me." Taking the plates to the sink she began to rinse the dishes.

Before she knew it, Jake had placed his arms on both sides of her and started kissing her on the neck. Turning into his arms she wrapped her arms around his neck and teasingly kissed his jaw. The dishes forgotten, Rachel felt the flame of desire spiral through her. Looking into his eyes she saw his desire for her was just as strong. She pressed against his firm body as she unbuttoned his shirt and kissed his chest.

Leaning his head against hers he asked, "Are you sure you want to do this?" Feeling her nodding her head yes, he tilted her face up with his finger to look into her eyes to see if she really meant it. Seeing the reflection of his own desire in her eyes he smiled and took her by the hand. Leading her through the obstacle course in the hallway, he put his arm around her as they climbed the stairs to the bedroom.

Stopping long enough to light a candle on the nightstand, Jake pulled her back into his arms. As he kissed her, one hand ran through her long silky hair while the other hand softly caressed her small firm breast. Unable to control their passion any longer they silently undressed each other. Finally with nothing left between them, Jake picked her up and placed her on the bed. Committing every inch of her body to memory he stood looking at her in the candlelight. Her skin flushing from the adoration showing on his face, Rachel held out her hand to him. Joining his hand in hers, he lay down beside her. His tongue tracing the curve of her neck, he could feel Rachel shiver with desire. With mounting passion Jake rolled on top of her and kissed his way down to her breast. His mouth suckled tenderly on one breast then the other, while his hands explored the rest of her. His fingers caressed the curves of her body and she gave herself freely and wantonly. Jake could feel the heat of passion soar through her as he touched her thigh, making her shudder with unreleased pleasure. Teasing her with his fingers, he brushed the soft hair that covered her womanhood. Unable to bear the hunger for him any longer she caught his hand in hers and moaned. Fully seduced by Rachel's beauty he raised his mouth from her breast and kissed her lips as he entered her.

Rachel had not been a virgin since college, but with Jake she felt like this was the first time for her. Riding the waves of passion as they swelled inside her, he took her higher than she ever knew was possible. Fire raced through her body, and looking into his silver eyes she felt their souls reach out to one another, and together they raced among the stars. One bright glowing star playfully called to them and they flew faster and faster until they reached it. Together they embraced the warmth of the star and smiled, knowing they were experiencing something as old as time. The heat of their passion grew stronger as they embraced the star, and suddenly it exploded into millions of tiny sparkling stars. The glistening star fragments gathered underneath them forming a golden cloud, and gently they floated back to earth. Their desire quenched, Rachel felt her soul return to her body and she held Jake until their breathing returned to normal. Rolling onto his side, Jake pulled Rachel closer to him and wrapped his arm around her. Her soft hair spilled out behind her as he tenderly kissed her again.

Her heart fluttering in her chest, Rachel told herself to be careful. She knew it would be too easy to fall in love with this man.

Silently reprimanding himself for being careless, he tried to think of a way to apologize to Rachel for not using a condom. He knew he would have to be more careful next time.

Gently touching his face, Rachel turned his head toward the light. Unable to read his expression she asked, "Jake, what's wrong?" Afraid he regretted making love to her, she sat up and looked at him.

Recognizing the hurt on her face, he pulled her back into his embrace and said, "Nothing's wrong, I just…well, I'm sorry I was careless. I promise I won't be next time."

Rubbing her fingertips lightly over the lower part of his stomach she said, "Oh, you mean there is more?"

Laughing, he reached down and pulled her hand up to his chest, holding it tight. "You keep that up and it will be sooner than later!"

"And what's wrong with sooner?" she asked.

Releasing his hold on her hand he leaned over her to the nightstand and pulled out a foil packet from the top drawer. Smiling wickedly at her he said, "You make a good point."

This time as he made love to her, Rachel knew she had never really made love to a man. His experience showed as he taught her how to please him. Finally, with the candle burning low, they slept.

Sometime in the early hours of the morning, with the last of the moon shining through the window, they were awakened by the ringing of the phone. Reaching over Rachel, Jake answered it. After listening for a minute he sat up, saying, "What! How long ago? Is anyone hurt?"

Hearing the alarm in Jake's voice Rachel slid out of bed and began to get dressed. Thinking he was being called to an accident, she thought she'd better get home. Her grandmother was going to be angry with her for staying out so late.

Hanging up the phone, Jake started dressing as quickly as he could. Seeing that she was almost dressed, he stopped her saying, "Rachel, wait, I'm going with you."

"Sounds like you need to go to work to me. Call me tomorrow, okay?"

"You don't understand," he said, pulling her toward the bed and sitting down beside her. "That call...there's been an explosion at your place. The volunteer fire department is on the way. We need to hurry."

Jumping up and grabbing her shoes, Rachel ran out of the room and down the stairs before he could catch her. Stopping her at the front door, he said, "You are in no condition to drive. Get in my Blazer, I'm driving!" Not arguing, she did as she was told.

CHAPTER NINE

Heading northeast out of Evergreen Jake turned on his siren when they were out of the city limits. The only other noise was the continuous squawk of his police radio. Afraid that Rachel might hear something she was not ready to hear Jake turned the radio down. As they drove closer to the farm they could see a faint orange glow in the distance. Knowing this was the glow from the fire at the farm, Rachel gasped. Thinking she may already be going into shock, Jake took her hand in his and silently offered his support. Her icy cold hand was another sign that she might be going into shock. Reaching the lane to the farm, Jake had to slow down and let a fire truck go by. Following behind the truck he drove up the hill toward the farmhouse.

Relief passed through both Rachel and Jake as they drew closer. It wasn't the main house that was on fire; the fire truck continued past the house toward the chicken house. Turning off his siren and stopping at the back of the house, he jumped out and stopped Rachel as she started to run down the lane. Holding her back he said, "Rachel, baby you can't do anything down there. Let the firemen do their job."

A movement on the back porch of the house caught his eye. Turning he saw Sherry, Barbara and Dora standing there, watching the destruction below. Jake really needed to go see what had happened, but he was afraid Rachel would follow him. Placing his arm around her shoulder, he guided her toward the porch and up the steps. "What happened, do you know?" he asked. The ladies all shook their heads no at the same time. Pushing Rachel toward Sherry, Jake said, "Here, take care of her. I'm going down there." Seeing the look on Rachel's face he kissed her quickly on the cheek. Turning to Dora he added, "It may be a long night...why don't you put some coffee on for everyone?"

*　*　*　*　*

Taking control of the group of women, Barbara said, "Of course, go. Just send us some word when you can to let us know how bad it is." Opening the back door she stood back as Sherry took Rachel inside. Once inside, all three could see the fright on

Rachel's face. Sherry too, thought Rachel might be in shock. Leading her to the table she sat Rachel down and offered Dora a hand with the coffee.

In no time the kitchen smelled like a coffee shop. Not only did Dora put on some coffee, she started frying bacon and sausage also. While the meat was cooking she pulled out the flour bowl and buttermilk and started making biscuits. When the coffee was ready, Sherry poured them all some. Taking a cup to Rachel she sat it down in front of her and said, "Rachel, drink some. It might help."

The innocent remark made Rachel's blood boil. Jumping up from the table she paced as she ranted, "Help! How is that supposed to help? What is going on? Who is doing this to us? You tell me how coffee is going to help, when there's a crazy person out there trying to kill us. First it was Aunt Darlyn, then me, who's next?" Her anger finally vented, she burst into tears. Sherry stopped her before she could run out of the room. Pulling Rachel into her arms, she comforted her.

Sensing that Rachel was gaining control of herself, Sherry stood back and looked at her. "Now, will you drink some coffee? It may be a while before Jake comes back to tell us what happened." Shaking her head yes, she went to the table and stirred some sugar into her cup.

After taking a sip of the steaming brew, Rachel half smiled and said, "Sorry, I guess I kind of lost it for a minute." Reassuring herself as well as the others in the room, she continued, "I'm all right now." Taking her grandmother's and her mother's hands in hers she smiled saying, "We're all going to be all right because, after all, hens rule! They're tough old birds, just like us."

Trying to keep Rachel's spirits up, Barbara gave her a regal stare and said, "Whom are you calling an old bird, young lady?"

Seeing the look on Barbara's face, both Sherry and Rachel started laughing almost hysterically. A knock at the back door made them stop and turn around. Dora answered the door and seeing Jake standing there let him in. His clothes were smudged with soot and ash from the fire, and he smelled like smoke, but Rachel thought he was the best looking man she had ever seen. Running into his arms, she said, "Well, tell us something! How bad is it?"

Hugging her close he replied, "I have good news and bad news. The good news is the actual chicken house is fine, and so are the hens. The bad news is the incinerator is a total loss."

"The incinerator? Is that what exploded? But how? I mean we haven't used it since last week." Confusion showed on Rachel's face.

*　　*　　*　　*　　*

Thinking that her many facial expressions were just one of the things that he loved about her, Jake said, "That's what Ollie just told me. The fire marshal will be combing over the rubble when it gets light out. He should be able to tell us what happened."

Interrupting their conversation, Barbara said to Jake, "Come sit down and have a cup of coffee, Jake. Dora, if those biscuits are done he'll have some of them too."

Pulling Jake toward the table, Rachel didn't give him an opportunity to refuse. Sitting down beside him she said, "Have the firemen got the fire completely out?"

Taking a bite of the hot buttered biscuit, Jake swallowed before he answered. "Not completely, and they will have to stay around for a while to make sure there are no hot spots. You know, nothing left that will flare back up." Filling another biscuit with some bacon he ate it too.

Seeing Jake devour the food in front of him, Barbara looked at Dora and asked, "Dora, do you have enough to take down to the firemen?"

"Yes, ma'am. There should be plenty, but I'll need help carrying it all."

Standing up, Barbara said, "Well, between all of us we should be able to carry it. Feeding them

some breakfast is the least we can do for their
heroic work tonight."

Agreeing, they all got up to help.

* * * * *

By mid morning word had spread about the fire
and everyone who knew them had either come by
or phoned to check on them. Staying at the house,
Barbara and Dora took the phone calls while
Rachel and Sherry spoke to anyone who came by.
The fire marshal was climbing through the ashes
and every once in a while he would pick something
up and look at it. He either placed it in a plastic
baggie and marked it, or he threw it back down
where he found it. Finally, with something in his
hand he walked toward Rachel and Jake.

Seeing him approach, Jake addressed him,
"Did you find something, Chief?"

His hands covered in soot, the chief answered,
"Yes, see this?" Showing Jake the piece of burnt
and twisted metal he continued, "That's what's left
of the thermostat. Look at it and you can see that
it's stuck. It seems to me that someone turned the
gas on high, closed the ventilation ducts, and blew
out the pilot light, leaving it like that. It didn't take
long for the gas to build up in the room. When
there was enough gas built up in the room some
kind of spark was set off and that is what made it
explode. I'm still looking for the trigger." Turning

to Rachel he asked, "When was the last time anyone used the incinerator?"

"About a week ago; we haven't been in there since."

"Well somebody was in there yesterday. Like I said, it didn't take the gas long to build up in there. My guess is about six or seven hours and there would be enough gas in the room to cause this kind of explosion. It's a good thing that the incinerator was connected to a propane tank by itself. If that had been connected to a natural gas line to the house, everything would have blown up."

"So you definitely are saying this was no accident?" asked Rachel.

"Accident? No, ma'am, no way this was an accident," he replied.

Handing the thermostat back to the chief, Jake said, "Thanks; when do you think your report will be ready?"

"I'll have it on your desk by this afternoon," the chief said as he turned and walked away.

Looking at Jake, Rachel asked, "Now what?"

Thinking before he answered her, Jake finally said, "I need to catch whoever is behind this before someone gets killed, that's what." Kissing her quickly on the mouth, he said, "I need to speak to Oscar, and then I better get to the office. I'll see you later."

"I'm going to hold you to that," she said.

Walking over to Oscar, Jake asked Sherry to excuse them and the two men walked toward Jake's Blazer while they talked. Reaching her mother's side, Rachel watched the men and said, "I wonder what that's all about."

"He's probably asking Oscar to keep an eye on us po' little women folk," Sherry answered with as much southern drawl as she could put into it. Laughing with her mother, Rachel agreed.

Waving as Jake drove away, Rachel told Sherry that she was going to the house and asked if she was coming. "You go ahead, I'll wait until Oscar is ready," Sherry replied.

* * * * *

Cussing under his breath, the man was again watching the scene below. He was supposed to meet with the boss in about an hour and give him a report on what was happening. Leaving by the old dirt road the man reflected on what they had tried over the last several weeks. The boss was still mad about the last screw up. He was going to be furious about this one. Once again their plan had failed. The fire was supposed to take out the chicken houses too, not just the incinerator. That would have put those ladies out of business, and his boss would have been able to buy the property real cheap. Thinking to himself that this place was jinxed, the man wanted to tell his boss to forget about this one and leave it alone. But, he knew that he wouldn't. His boss was even meaner and crazier than he was. Being honest with himself, the man realized he was afraid of the boss.

Reaching his cabin the man saw the boss's car parked under the trees. This place was so far back in the woods, no one could see the cabin. He didn't understand why the boss thought he needed to hide his car. Going inside, the man was suddenly hit in the head. Staggering against the door he looked at the boss but didn't say anything. Waiting to see if he was going to get hit again, he looked around the room for something to defend himself with. Nothing was in reach so he prepared to block the next blow when it came. Instead of hitting the man again, the boss yelled at him, "You don't have to tell me—I know you blew it again! Hell, the whole town knows about it already!" Seeing that the man was about to make excuses he said, "And don't you say you're sorry! I'm the one who should be sorry for trusting you do get the job done!" The man stood by the door, not moving, and watched as the boss ranted and paced around the small one room cabin. After a few minutes the boss stopped pacing and, turning around, smiled at the man. Knowing the boss was his most dangerous when he was friendly made the man cringe inside. Still smiling the boss said, "Well, don't just stand there like an idiot, come on and sit down. I'll tell you what we're going to do now. I was hoping it wouldn't come to this, but we don't have a choice now." Slowly walking to the old table and sitting across from the boss, the man listened to their next plan of action.

* * * * *

A week had gone by since the fire and things were starting to get back to normal around the farm. During the week Ollie helped Juan and Maria in the chicken house, and on the weekends he helped Rachel with the garden. Sherry and Barbara had settled down into a routine of household chores, surprising Rachel by their lack of arguing. Rachel had been busy that week making arrangements to have a new incinerator built and keeping the county health department from shutting her down. Thankful for the peace at home she was able to concentrate on business.

The afternoon sun was shining on Rachel's back as she started walking down the dirt lane toward the mailbox: She had seen the mail lady go by when she was working in the garden earlier. As she walked back to the house she shuffled through the mail, noting that it was mostly bills. The last envelope was large and thick. Reading the return address first, she saw that it was from a pharmaceutical company in Birmingham, and was addressed to her Aunt Darlyn. She decided the mail could wait and put it on the desk in the study.

Hearing voices coming up the hall from the kitchen Rachel went to see who was there. Barbara and Dora were sitting at the table drinking ice tea and eating a piece of apple pie. Joining them at the table she picked at the crust on the pie and asked, "Where is Mama?"

Exchanging a smile with Dora, Barbara answered her, "Where do you think she is? Sherry is with Oscar of course. She has been spending a lot of her time with him lately."

Sighing, Rachel said, "Yea, I know."

"Are you still worried about him? I told you I'd tell you what I know about his background if it's worrying you that much."

"And I told you I don't want to know what your private investigator had to say."

Reaching over and tapping Rachel's hand away from the pie, Dora spoke up saying, "Well, don't listen to what your grandmother has to say, but leave that pie alone or get a plate and cut yourself a piece."

Rachel had not been aware that she was even picking at the pie until Dora tapped her on the hand. Embarrassed, she put her hands in her lap.

Susan Weekley

She wasn't really hungry, she was nervous. Realizing this, a bad feeling came over her.

Seeing Rachel fidget made Barbara ask, "What's really bothering you Rachel?"

Looking at her grandmother and Dora she slowly answered, "I'm not sure, but I have a bad feeling, like something awful is going to happen. I can't shake it."

Seeing the anxiety on Rachel's face and hearing it in her voice, Barbara tried to reassure her that it was because of everything that had already happened. "I'm confident that your young man will find the person responsible for what is happening and arrest him real soon."

Hearing her grandmother refer to Jake as her young man made Rachel blush at the memory of their night alone together. Smiling at the memory, she said, "You are probably right. Speaking of my young man, I have a date with him tonight, so I guess I'd better get ready."

As she started up the stairs, Rachel could hear bits and pieces of the conversation between her grandmother and Dora. Hearing her name mentioned she stopped on the stairs just out of sight and listened as Dora said, "When are you going to tell her the truth?"

"Not until she is ready. She's had enough to deal with this week."

"You're going to have to tell her sometime, and sooner is better than later."

"I know, and I'll tell her, I promise."

The buzzer going off on the dryer in the laundry room stopped their conversation and Rachel could hear no more. Afraid she would be caught eavesdropping Rachel eased up the rest of the stairs and went to her room. Not understanding the conversation between the two women, Rachel dismissed it from her mind.

After her shower she glanced at the clock to see how much time she had before Jake would be there to pick her up. Roxanne was throwing a small dinner party and had invited them to come. She was going to have to hurry if she was going to be ready on time.

Rachel was ready when Jake arrived for their date. However, her grandmother had taught her at an early age to never meet her date at the door…'a lady always keeps them waiting' was her motto.

Jake was standing at the parlor doors talking to Barbara when Rachel came down the stairs. His eyes lit up at the sight of her. Rachel was wearing the spring green pants suit she had bought at Christi's boutique. Her hair was pulled up in a French twist with a few spiraling curls in front and back. Small pearl earrings dangled from each ear. Thinking again that she was the most beautiful woman he had ever seen he said, "Good evening, Rachel. You look wonderful tonight."

Kissing Jake softly on the mouth, Rachel said thank you. Stepping back and looking closer at him she said, "You look pretty handsome yourself tonight." Sniffing, she added, "And you smell good too." Jake had not been sure what to wear to this little dinner party so he dressed up in his best black pants and a gray dress shirt. Thinking a tie was too formal he opted not to wear one.

"Are you ready to go?" he asked.

Nodding her head yes, they said good night to Barbara and headed for the party. It was a short distance to Roxanne and Ollie's house. In fact it was just down Highway 31, about a mile or so. Jake and Rachel didn't have much time to talk before they arrived.

Ollie greeted them at the door saying, "Come on in." When they stepped into the living room Rachel was surprised to see Maria playing with Molly. Curiosity was killing Rachel, but she didn't ask Ollie how long he had been seeing Maria.

Coming out of the kitchen, Roxanne said, "Hey, I'm glad ya'll are here. I hope you like spaghetti. It will be ready soon."

Teasing his older sister, Ollie said, "Yea, I hope you like it too! She made enough for an army!" Laughing he continued, "Jake if you don't help me eat it, I'll be having it for supper every night this week!"

Before Jake could respond there was a knock at the door. Looking at Roxanne in surprise Ollie asked, "Who can that be?"

Smiling wickedly at her brother, Roxanne said, "My date." Not giving Ollie a chance to question her, Roxanne rushed to the door.

Still standing with her arm linked in Jake's, Rachel felt him tense when Alec walked in on Roxanne's arm.

Smiling broadly at the group Roxanne said, "Alec, you know everyone don't you?"

Looking at Maria and Molly he said no he didn't. After Roxanne introduced Maria and Molly to Alec she turned to Ollie and said, "Ollie, don't just stand there looking like you been hit with a stupid stick! Get everyone something to drink!" Excusing herself saying she needed to check on the bread, Roxanne went back into the kitchen.

Ollie followed her and, taking a couple of beers from the refrigerator, he looked at her and said, "This should be an interesting night!" Removing the bread from the oven Roxanne thought to herself that she was counting on it.

The conversation was sparse at first, but finally everyone settled into a rhythm of topics. The men discussed sports while the women tried to keep

Molly out of trouble. After a few minutes Roxanne said supper was ready if they were.

Ollie led Maria and Molly into the dining room and helped each of them with their chair. Neither Ollie nor Maria missed it when Jake practically bumped Alec out of the way as they both tried to pull out a chair for Rachel. Pretending not to notice, Rachel sat down in the middle chair, leaving Jake on one side of her and Alec on the other. This left Roxanne a place at the head of the table next to Alec and Maria.

As they ate Roxanne worked at keeping the conversation flowing. After exhausting every subject she could think of she said, "So, Jake, have you gotten any leads on Rachel's attacker?"

Jake had been dreading the moment but he knew it would come up sometime tonight. Setting his fork down he said, "Roxanne, you know I can't discuss police business with any of you."

Seizing the chance to make Jake look bad in front of Rachel, Alec interrupted, "Oh come on, Sheriff, surely you have some sort of lead—or is this going in the records as an unsolved crime?"

Barely keeping his anger under control Jake replied, "No, it's not going on the record as unsolved. My department is working night and day on this case!"

Feeling the tension on both sides of her, Rachel calmly said to Alec, "I have complete faith in Jake, and I know he will find the person responsible for my attack. Now if you gentlemen don't mind, I don't care to hear any more about it tonight."

Sorry she had brought the subject up Roxanne asked, "Who wants dessert?"

Ollie answered saying, "Molly and I do, don't we, my girl?"

Smiling sweetly at her daddy she said, "Yes, Roxy made cake!" The child's innocence brought a sense of shame over Jake and Alec, both of them agreeing that cake sounded good to them too.

"Well then, if you ladies will help me take these dishes to the kitchen, we'll get the dessert. You men can be getting the table ready for a game of cards."

Grabbing as many plates as they could carry, the three women went into the kitchen. As soon as the door was closed Maria looked at Roxanne and said, "Man, I thought for sure those two were going to tie up in there! Why did you invite Alec?"

Setting dessert dishes on a tray with the chocolate cake she had made, Roxanne turned and looked at both Maria and Rachel as she answered, "Look, I know he is younger than me and everything, but I keep hoping that someday my prince charming will walk into my life. At my age I can't be picky…I have to entertain any available bachelor I can find. Alec came into the shop yesterday for a haircut, so I invited him. I didn't want to be the only one here tonight without a date." Sighing she added, "Rachel, I'm sorry if Alec being here has made things between you and Jake difficult. I didn't know Alec had the hots for you."

Laughing, Maria said, "Yeah, it's been obvious to all of us that Jake is jealous."

Smiling at that, Rachel said, "I know; I thought I would like him being jealous over me, but I have to admit that his constant touching me is getting on my nerves. He kept playing footsie under the table with me or brushing his hand against mine while we ate."

Giggling at Rachel's remark, Roxanne finished arranging the dessert tray and said, "Sounds like Jake's got it bad."

The kitchen door opened and Ollie walked in whispering, "If you ladies don't hurry up I'm not going to be responsible for what those two roosters do in there." Looking at Ollie as if they didn't understand, he added, "Well okay, but if any furniture gets broken, Roxanne, you're paying for it." Saying that he walked out of the kitchen.

"Oh no, I'll go see what's happened," said Rachel.

"Me too," said Maria.

Following the others out of the kitchen balancing the tray carefully, Roxanne walked into the dining room just in time to see Jake punch Alec in the face. Not having time to get out of the way Alec landed on top of her, knocking them both to the floor. Covered in cake, Alec sat there and looked at everyone. Instead of getting up and going after Jake he started laughing. "Guess I deserved that." Turning and helping Roxanne off the floor he continued, "Roxanne, I'm sorry I ruined your party. I hope you will let me make it up to you and take you out to dinner sometime."

Wiping cake off her face, she looked around the room at everyone's faces and said to Alec, "Sure, dinner would be nice."

So angry with Jake for his behavior, Rachel spoke up saying, "Roxanne, I'm sorry about all this, but I think Jake and I should be leaving."

"It's okay, I'll call you tomorrow," Roxanne replied.

Taking Jake by the hand Rachel pulled him from the room. When they were safely outside, Rachel stopped Jake and asked, "Do you mind telling me what that was all about? Why did you have to hit him?"

Disgusted and still angry, Jake stormed to the Blazer and got in, slamming the door. Rushing to get in, thinking he was going to leave her, Rachel jumped in and slammed her door. "Oh, no you're not just driving away without giving me an explanation!" Starting the Blazer and peeling out of the driveway with rocks flying, Jake started toward town.

He was driving so fast that Rachel got scared on top of being angry. "Slow down, Jake you're going to get us killed!" she yelled as she grabbed hold of the dashboard.

Still angry but sorry he had scared her, Jake slowed down and pulled off the highway onto a dirt lane. Before Rachel knew what was happening Jake had pulled her into his arms, roughly kissing her. Bruising her lips, he started pulling at her buttons. At first she kissed him back, but the rougher he got the angrier she got. Finally pushing him away from her, she yelled "Stop right now! You aren't touching me again until you tell me what's going on!"

"I couldn't stand the way that jerk was looking at you all night! He knew you were there with me! He kept hassling me about your attack while you were in the kitchen. Just wouldn't stop saying things like, 'Maybe I needed to call the state police to see if they could solve the case'. He did everything he could to make me look bad in front of you."

"So instead of ignoring him, you hit him? That was supposed to make you look good to me? Men! You're all nuts! Take me home!"

Not saying another word they both rode the rest of the way to MacKinstry Farm in silence. Stopping in front of the house, Jake was ready to apologize for his behavior, but before he could do it, Rachel jumped out of the Blazer and ran up the steps into the house.

Immediately going upstairs to her room, she slammed the bedroom door. Getting ready for bed she tried to calm down; Jake had scared her with his jealousy. Crawling under the covers she cried herself to sleep.

* * * * *

Jake's mood was no better by the time he reached his house. Taking a beer onto the back deck he leaned against the rail and thought about what he had done. The beer was not setting well on his stomach, so he poured it out and threw the bottle away. Climbing the stairs to his room he remembered the night Rachel had spent with him. With heavy footsteps, he too went to bed.

Restlessly both Jake and Rachel slept, their dreams filled with images of each other and the love they shared. Their hearts were breaking as they longed to be in each other's arms.

Susan Weekley

CHAPTER TEN

The next morning Rachel was awakened by the ringing of the telephone. Praying that someone else would get it, she pulled the pillow out from under her head and covered her ears in an attempt to block the noise. After two rings it stopped. Saying a prayer of thanks to whoever answered the phone she pulled the pillow back under her head and tried to go back to sleep. Her rest was short lived. A knock at her bedroom door made her jump. Sitting up in bed she moaned, "Come in."

Silently the door swung open enough for Dora to stick her head in and say, "Sorry to wake you, Ms. Rachel, but Ms. Roxanne is on the phone and asking to speak to you."

Reaching for the telephone on the nightstand, Rachel told Dora thank you before she left the room. Rachel had been expecting to hear from Roxanne today, but not this early. She knew

Roxanne would want to talk about what happened after she and Jake left her house last night. Not ready to face her emotions about last night she placed the receiver in her lap, sat up further in the bed and adjusted the covers around her. Hesitating long enough to take a deep breath, she picked up the receiver and teasingly said, "I finally get a day to sleep late and you have to call this early? It better be good!"

Laughing at Rachel's greeting, Roxanne answered, "When there is a four year old in the house, eight thirty is late. I've been up since six. You are too young to be sleeping the day away." The only response Roxanne got out of Rachel was a grunt of disapproval. "Well, anyway, I called to see if you wanted to get together for lunch today—maybe do a little shopping. You know, a girls day out." Deciding this sounded like fun, Rachel agreed to meet Roxanne at the diner around noon.

No sooner had Rachel hung up the phone when it rang again. Answering it quickly so it would not disturb anyone else in the house, she said, "Hello."

"Rachel? Hi, this is Christi Reynolds. I hope I haven't called too early. How are you this morning?"

Surprised to hear from Christi, Rachel answered, "I'm fine Christi. You sound wired this morning. What's going on?"

"I need a major favor! Would it be possible for you to come by the shop this afternoon? My daughter is gone on a school field trip and I have to finish a wedding gown by tomorrow. You said you might be a model for me."

Excited over this idea, Rachel said, "I'd love to. Roxanne and I are planning on coming by the shop after lunch. Will that be okay?"

"That's perfect. You don't know how much this will mean to me!"

"Christi, I do have one question. Why aren't you using the bride for this fitting?"

Laughing, Christi said, "Oh, there isn't a bride. This is the wedding dress in my fall line I'm unveiling at a fashion show next week. I have to have it finished by tomorrow so it can be packed and shipped to New Orleans."

"Oh. Okay; well I'll see you after lunch."

"I'll be ready for you. Thanks, see you then."

Hanging up the phone Rachel told herself she was not even going to think about Jake today. She had a busy schedule to keep and intended to have a good time with her girlfriends.

Over a light lunch of tuna salad on fresh croissants Roxanne asked the question Rachel had been expecting to hear since she arrived. "So, are you going to keep me in suspense forever? Tell me what happened after you and Jake left last night!"

Shrugging her shoulders, Rachel said, "What's to tell? He took me home and I haven't heard from him since."

Recognizing the hurt in Rachel's voice for what it was, Roxanne said, "Oh, I'm sorry Rachel. Did the two of you get in a fight or something?"

Needing to vent some of her frustrations, Rachel broke down and told Roxanne everything that had happened between her and Jake. Speaking of Jake, she realized just how strong her feelings for him had become in such a short period of time. Thinking she sounded like a lovesick adolescent she attempted to change the subject. "So, now it's your turn. Tell me what happened between you and Alec after we left. And how long have Ollie and Maria been seeing each other?"

"Ollie and Maria started dating about two weeks ago. They look so good together. Did you know Maria is an excellent cook? She also seems to be well educated for a migrant worker. I really don't know much about her. She's good with Molly though, and that means a lot to Ollie. I think if my little brother plays his cards right, I just might have a new sister-in-law; one I can stand to be around!"

"That's great! I have to admit I was surprised to see the two of them together, but Maria is a nice person and I think they look good together as a couple. I hope everything works out okay for them." Finishing the last of her lunch and drinking a sip of her ice tea, Rachel realized that Roxanne had not mentioned Alec. Setting her glass down on the table she looked Roxanne in the eye and said, "Now, what happened between you and Alec? And don't say nothing, I can see by the look in your eyes that something did!"

Roxanne waited to respond to Rachel, as the waitress had picked this moment to ask if they were through with their lunch. She sat there and smiled while the waitress cleared the table and left the check. Unable to suppress her excitement any longer, Roxanne exclaimed, "You are so much like your Aunt Darlyn! I can't get anything past you."

"I knew it! Tell all!" Rachel prompted.

"Well, after you and Jake left and I changed clothes, Alec was still there. He apologized for being rude to Jake and causing problems between you two. He asked me to go to the movies tonight with him." Smiling coyly, she added, "And he kisses like a dream!"

Ignoring the part about how Alec kisses, Rachel asked, "Are you going?"

"Hell, yeah, I'm going! Do you know how long it's been since I went on a real date?" Not waiting for Rachel to answer her question she continued, "That's why I wanted you to come shopping with me. I need something really nice to wear!"

Laughing at her friend's enthusiasm, Rachel said, "Well, let's go see what we can find at Homespun & More. I'm sure we will find the perfect outfit for you."

Paying the tab the two ladies left the diner.

* * * * *

The day after Roxanne's party, Jake felt lousy. He knew he had not been honest with Rachel and his guilty conscience bothered him all day. He had been jealous of the attention Rachel had been giving Alec. Jealousy was a new experience for Jake and he did not like it, but as bad as he felt he could not bring himself to call Rachel and apologize.

Needing to get out of the office for a while Jake agreed to go pick up some lunch for Karen at the diner. He wasn't getting any work done anyway. His mind kept wandering back to the fight he and Rachel had the night before.

Parking his Blazer in the diner parking lot, he made it as far as the sidewalk and ran into Bonnie Banks.

"Well, good morning, Jake. How are you today?"

Forcing a smile he said, "I'm fine, Bonnie. How about you?"

"I'm fine." Sticking her bottom lip out in an exaggerated pout, she continued. "But now that I think about it I'm mad at you."

Jake was in no mood for Bonnie's games but since she was a member of the city council he had no choice but to be nice to her. Still smiling he asked, "Well, whatever for?"

"You left me at the barbecue all by myself. Remember?"

Chuckling he replied, "If I remember correctly, I left you with Alec. From what I hear most of the females around here find him very attractive and would have enjoyed spending time in his company."

Running her forefinger along the side of his chin, Bonnie gave her most coquettish smile and said, "In case you haven't noticed, I'm not like most females."

Tiring of this game Jake tried to excuse himself saying, "I'm in a hurry. Karen is waiting on her lunch. I'll talk to you later." Turning he started for the door of the diner.

Not intending to let him get away so easily, Bonnie linked her arm through his and walked down the sidewalk with him. Ignoring his brush off she said, "Will I see you tonight?"

Curiosity getting the best of Jake, he stopped and looked at her questionably.

Understanding the look on Jake's face she said, "Don't tell me you've forgotten about the party at the mayor's house tonight."

Not wanting to admit that he had, Jake assured her he had not forgotten and that he would see her there. The last thing Jake wanted to do was attend a stuffy formal dinner party, but he could think of no way out of it. Resigned to the day ahead he walked on toward the diner with Bonnie in tow.

Rachel was beginning to enjoy the day until she turned the corner and ran straight into Jake. Seeing Bonnie draped on his arm made her green eyes darker with jealousy. Both Jake and Rachel were taken by surprise and neither could find the words to say anything. Coming up behind Rachel, Roxanne said, "Well hey Jake, Bonnie. Are you two going in for lunch?"

Smiling serenely Bonnie replied, "Yes, I've been trying to persuade Jake to join me—"

Finding his voice, Jake cut Bonnie off before the situation got out of control and left Rachel with the wrong impression. "Now Bonnie, I told you I can't stay. I only came by to pick up an order that Karen called in. I have to get back to work." Pulling his arm free from her grasp he looked at Rachel and said, "May I talk to you a minute?"

Not ready to talk to Jake alone, Rachel shook her head no, saying, "Roxanne and I have things to do. We can talk later." With that she turned and walked across the parking lot with Roxanne following closely at her heels.

Getting into Roxanne's car, Rachel glanced to see where Jake was. What she saw only made her heart ache. Bonnie had latched onto Jake again and was going into the diner with him as they pulled out of the parking lot.

*   *   *   *   *

No matter how she tried to hide her breaking heart Roxanne knew Rachel was hurting. Attempting to lift Rachel's spirits Roxanne said, "Bonnie doesn't stand a chance of ever getting Jake's attention. She is a money hungry she-devil and Jake knows it!"

Rachel didn't want to talk about Jake; however, she was curious about Bonnie. "Has she really been married three times?"

"Oh, yes! Each time she married to a man richer than the one before him. I guess maybe she's finally got enough money that she doesn't need to marry anyone else who's rich. It's either that or she just feels like slumming it with the working class for a while. Lord knows Jake don't make the kind of money she has!" Parking the car in front of the dress shop, Roxanne looked at Rachel and said, "Come on. Let's go have some fun! I can't wait to see you in this wedding dress Christi has designed!"

Lifting her eyebrow in surprise Rachel asked, "How did you know Christi asked me to model for her?"

Roxanne answered her as she got out of the car. "Christi called me after she called you this morning. She wanted to thank me for introducing the two of you."

Both Sara and Christi greeted them when they entered the dress shop. Roxanne went with Sara to find something to wear on her date. Sara was so excited for Roxanne she could not stop asking questions, like where they were going, and how they had met.

Christi showed Rachel to her workroom behind the cash register. The room served as both design area and sewing room. An invisible line clearly separated the room in half. Bolts of every kind of fabric, lace, buttons, and other materials needed for sewing were lined up in adjustable shelves along the larger wall. A commercial size sewing machine was placed on this side of the room. A modeling stand had been placed behind the sewing machine. On the other side of the room was a drafting table with colored pencils. All the latest fashion magazines were there.

Smiling at Rachel, Christi said, "Welcome to my lair!"

Wondering what she had gotten herself into, Rachel went behind the dressing screen and took her clothes off as Christi had instructed. Christi handed her a long full slip and she put it on before she came out. Feeling self-conscious, she walked to the fitting stand and stepped onto it. Before she knew it Christi had thrown the wedding gown over her head and went to work. Tucking and pulling at the gown, Christi didn't give Rachel much of a chance to see what the gown looked like. Rachel realized talking would be difficult for Christi since she had a mouth full of pins so she stood there and listened to the conversation in the front room. Hearing Sara ring up a sale Rachel knew Roxanne had found what she was looking for.

The ringing of the bell over the front door let Rachel know someone else had come into the shop. Thinking to herself, Rachel could see how the back room gave Sara and Christi a chance to hear the town gossip without anyone knowing they were there.

Paying for her new outfit, Roxanne looked up to see who had come in the door. Surprised to see Bonnie walking in her direction she said, "I thought you were eating lunch."

Looking like the cat that swallowed the bird, Bonnie smiled and said, "Oh, I just got a salad to go. I'll eat it in my office." Addressing Sara, she said, "I came by to pick up my dress for the party tonight. You said it would be ready."

Pulling a garment bag from the rack behind her, Sara said, "It's ready, Ms. Banks. What party did you say it was for?"

"The mayor and his wife are having a dinner party for the members of the city council. Of course all the county officials will be there as well."

"Do you have a date going with you?" asked Sara.

"No, but I did convince the mayor's wife to sit me next to the most handsome bachelor in town."

Laughing at Bonnie's remark, Sara asked, "And who might that be?"

"Why the sheriff, of course!" answered Bonnie. Holding the dress bag up she gave Sara a look of superiority and said, "Please put this on my bill." Not waiting for Sara to comment she left the shop.

Giving Bonnie a hateful stare, Roxanne said to Sara, "New dress or not she don't stand a snowballs chance in hell of getting Jake's attention."

Laughing Sara agreed, saying, "Yeah, the whole town has seen how she throws herself at him. What makes it so comical is that he hasn't shown the least bit of interest in her." Changing the subject she said, "Let's go see how Christi and Rachel are doing."

As soon as she walked through the curtain, Roxanne could tell by the look on Rachel's face that she had heard the conversation between Sara and Bonnie. Trying to take Rachel's mind off of Jake, she commented on the gown Christi was working on. Moving closer for a better look Roxanne smiled and said, "Oh, Christi, the gown is beautiful! Rachel, it looks like she made it especially for you!"

Sara and Christi pulled a large mirror in front of Rachel so she could get a good look at the dress. *Roxanne was right*, she thought, *the dress does look like it was made for me.* She was covered in white satin and handmade lace. Revealing the graceful line of Rachel's neck, the gown was rounded off the shoulders with sleeves snuggly fitting her arms and ending in a v-cut on the top of her hands. The empire waistband was covered with tiny white seed pearls. Lace and pearls flowed over the layer of satin underneath to the floor. Stunned by her own reflection Rachel said, "Oh! I look...I mean...Christi, it's gorgeous! I know if I were getting married this is the dress I would want."

Pleased that her friends liked her creation, Christi said, "Thank you, both, for your honesty. I just hope it looks this good on the model next week at the fashion show! No matter what I design models always try to change something on the garment at the last minute, trying to make it more them. You wouldn't believe how many times I have had dresses ruined."

Looking at herself one more time in the mirror Rachel said, "Christi, please promise me you won't let anything happen to this dress. I'll come to New Orleans and model it for you myself if I have too!"

"Don't worry about it, Rachel. I plan on protecting this dress and only selling it to someone who will do it justice."

Interrupting, Roxanne said, "Rachel, if you are through here I need to get moving. I have a date tonight, remember!"

Sara and Christi helped Rachel out of the wedding gown. Soon Roxanne and Rachel were on their way back to the diner to pick up Rachel's car. Telling Roxanne to call her tomorrow and let her know how the date went, Rachel went back to MacKinstry Farm.

At dinner that night Rachel kept drifting away in her own thoughts. Not ready to discuss what happened the night before or seeing Jake today at the diner, Rachel kept her feelings to herself.

Both Sherry and Barbara had heard her come in and slam her bedroom door last night. Without having to ask they knew Rachel and Jake must have had a lovers spat. While she was shopping with Roxanne, Sherry asked Barbara to leave her alone and let her work the problem out by herself. Agreeing, Barbara said she would give Rachel the privacy she needed.

*   *   *   *   *

Jake had no intention of staying long at the mayor's dinner party. Arriving late, he used the excuse that the case he was working on was keeping him busy. He had only been there long enough for one drink when dinner was announced. He took his seat, realizing too late that he had been placed next to Bonnie. He tried to keep his conversations with her brief but she was talking nonstop. The high pitch of her voice combined with the smell of her over-powering perfume was making him physically ill. The few times she was occupied by the councilman on her left, Jake's mind wandered back to the argument with Rachel last night. As soon as dinner was over, Jake made his excuses to the mayor's wife and left.

Now standing outside on his own deck, he remembered the night Rachel had spent with him. Reaching a decision, Jake knew what he had to do.

Smiling to himself, he admitted he was in love with Rachel. Tomorrow he would work on showing her.

CHAPTER ELEVEN

The next morning dawned just as sunny as the day before. Rachel had not slept well and was tired, so she stayed in her room. Hearing the clock downstairs strike noon, boredom got the best of her and she decided to take a walk. As she went out the back door she heard a car pulling out of the back driveway. Seeing her mother leaving she had no doubt Sherry was going to see Oscar again. Hard as she tried, Rachel could not understand why her mother was spending so much time with that man.

She stopped before entering the chicken house, changed her mind, and walked toward the woods.

June was already here, and thinking that the time she had spent at the farm since Darlyn's death had flown by, she entered the forest of tall southern pines and oak trees. With her eyes focused on the ground and watching for snakes she did not see the man hiding behind a tree about ten feet from her.

As she walked, she soon discovered a path in the woods. Wondering where it led she followed it. The path looked like it had been there a long time, and by the broken branches on some of the weeds and shrubs Rachel could tell someone had used it recently.

Suddenly, a cold chill ran down her spine. She could feel the presence of someone watching her from the woods. Quickly turning around, she looked to see if someone was behind her. Seeing no one, she tried to keep her fear from turning into panic, telling herself she was silly to be scared in broad daylight, until she remembered that her attack had happened during the day. Sudden terror seized her, and she ran back the way she had come, totally out of breath by the time she reached the chicken house. She slowed down to a walk and debated with herself whether or not to call Jake and tell him about her discovery. She just knew this had to be the way the person had come into the chicken house without being seen. When she reached the house, Rachel went to the study to call Jake. She started to dial the number, changed her mind and hung up before it started to ring. *No*, she thought, *he is going to have to call me and apologize for his behavior before I tell him about the path*. In the meantime, she would be more careful where she took her walks.

Satisfied with her decision, she picked up the mail that was piling up and started to take care of some of the bills. Opening and sorting the mail, she once again came across the envelope addressed to Darlyn from the pharmaceutical company. Curious, she opened the envelope. Glancing at the papers she could tell that it was a chemical report of some kind. Not understanding the report, she filed it in the desk drawer under miscellaneous.

* * * * *

Turning off Highway 31 into the park, Sherry did not see Oscar's car. Deciding it was too hot to wait inside her car until he arrived, she got out and headed for the riverbank. The parking lot had been empty so she had the park to herself. The sunlight reflecting off the water put Sherry in a peaceful mood. Walking along the river toward the bridge, Sherry had time to think about her relationship with Oscar. He was the most fascinating man she had ever met. Try as she might, she could not find one thing about him that would discourage her from seeing him. Walking under the bridge she could hear cars going overhead. They were louder than she thought they would be. Thinking that one of the cars might be Oscar, she turned and started back toward the picnic area. Suddenly she was caught from behind. A bag or sack of some kind came over her head so fast she could not see who had her. Struggling against her abductor she started to scream. A punch in the stomach cut the scream short and she lost her breath. A voice at her ear warned her not to scream, or there would be more where that came from. Heedful of his instructions she tried to keep up with him as he pulled her across the sand by one arm. Sherry used her free hand and managed to break the chain of the locket Oscar had given her a week ago. Dropping it on the riverbank, she prayed that Oscar would find it and know that something had happened to her.

*   *   *   *   *

Still in the study as the clock struck two, Rachel was about to go to the kitchen for a late lunch when there was a pounding on the front door. Opening the door, Rachel was surprised to see Oscar standing there…she thought he was with her mother. About to ask where Sherry was, Rachel realized that something was wrong; Oscar was white as a sheet. Barreling into the house, he asked if Sherry was home.

"No, she left about noon. I thought she was going to meet you."

"Oh, God. Oh, my God!" Running his hand through his hair he paced the foyer.

Trying to make sense of the situation, Rachel took Oscar by the arm and pulled him into the parlor. Getting him a drink of scotch, she asked, "Oscar, what's wrong? Where is my mother?"

"I don't know! We were supposed to meet at the park for a picnic. Her car was there when I arrived but I couldn't find her anywhere! The only thing I found was this!" Holding up the broken locket he explained that he had given it to Sherry last week. She had worn it every day after that. "I know something happened to her! She wouldn't have just left it lying by the river unless something was wrong!" Moaning again in anguish, he threw back the scotch and emptied the glass. Slowly, he regained his composure. He had tried so hard to believe that Sherry would be at the house, but deep down in his heart he knew she wouldn't be.

Fear spread through Rachel so fast she was paralyzed where she stood. Fortunately, Dora had been standing in the foyer and heard everything Oscar had said. Rushing into the room, she picked up the phone and started to call the sheriff's office. Oscar stopped her, saying he had already called on his cell phone and Jake was on his way there now. Placing the telephone in the cradle, Dora asked if she could get him another drink. Not waiting for an answer, she poured him another and one for Rachel. Taking the drinks to each of them she stood back and waited for someone to say something.

The ring of the telephone made all three of them jump. Frozen, Rachel just stared at it. When Dora started for it, again Oscar stopped her, saying, "Rachel, pull yourself together. You need to answer it. It might be the person who has your mother." Gently but firmly, he took her by the arm and pulled her toward the phone.

Her hands shaking as she picked up the receiver, she answered, "Hello." The voice on the other end made Rachel relax; shaking her head at Oscar, she silently told him it wasn't the kidnapper. "Hey, Roxanne. No, I'm fine. Yes, I'm still mad at Jake." She listened to Roxanne over the phone then cut in, trying to sound calm. "Listen, Roxanne, you kind of caught me in the middle of something. Can I call you back later tonight?" Again, she listened to the other end. "Okay, we'll talk later, bye." Ending her conversation, Rachel hung up the phone. Walking back to the coffee table where she had left her drink, she picked it up and swallowed. She felt the scotch burn her throat all the way down to her stomach. Slowly, it calmed the butterflies that had been fluttering in her stomach when she went to the phone. A knock at the door startled her, but she didn't jump this time.

"That's probably Jake," said Oscar. Following Dora to the door, Oscar met Jake and immediately asked, "Have you found Sherry?"

Walking into the parlor, Jake stiffened at the sight of Rachel. She was pale and looked like she was ready to collapse. Pulling her into his arms, Jake kissed her on the cheek and whispered, "I'm sorry about the other night." Taking her by the hand he pulled her to the love seat and sat down beside her. Looking at Oscar, he finally answered the question. "No, there is no sign of Sherry at the river. Her car was there just like you said, but she wasn't. I have my men searching the area."

Desperately trying to stay calm, Rachel asked, "Well, what do we do now?"

With a pained expression, Jake said the words Rachel did not want to hear. "All we can do right now is wait. She has to be missing for forty-eight hours before we can file a missing persons report on her with the state."

"That long? My God, anything could happen to her in that time!" Anger hit Rachel like a sledgehammer. She had to do something—she couldn't just sit here. Jumping up from the love seat, she began to pace. Her mind racing, she tried to think of something that would help.

Turning as she paced, Rachel almost ran into Dora. Placing her hand on Rachel's arm Dora said, "Ms. Rachel, please calm down. I just know Ms. Sherry will be all right. She is a resourceful and strong person, one who can take care of herself. It's your grandmother I'm worried about; I don't know if she can take any more bad news."

Reassuring the older woman, Rachel replied, "You're right, Dora. Mama knows how to take care of herself. And don't you worry about Grandmother. She's stronger than people think."

Listening to the conversation, Oscar prayed that the ladies were right. He knew Sherry was smart and would do what she needed to do to stay alive. Just then, the phone rang again. This time Rachel steadily walked to it and answered. With Jake standing at her side, she held the receiver so he could hear the other end. "Hello," she said.

"Ms. Collier?"

The voice was muffled and Rachel could not recognize it. "Yes, this is Ms. Collier."

"I have your mother. If you want to see her alive, you'll do as I say. Do you understand?"

Fear once again crept over Rachel, but so did anger. "Who is this? How do I know you have my mother?" she demanded.

"Shut up and listen carefully!" the voice boomed through the receiver. "I have your mother right here." Rachel could hear a noise on the other end then she heard Sherry say, "I'm okay, Rachel, just do as they say." Another noise and the man's voice came back on the line. "Now you know I wasn't lying to you. I'll call you back with your instructions so be ready at any time. And don't think about calling the police, Ms. Collier. Do you understand?"

"Yes. I under—"

"Good. Wait for my instructions!" Then the line went dead.

Taking the phone from Rachel, Jake hung it up, saying, "Well we don't have to wait forty-eight hours now. Contact has been made by the kidnappers, so we can inform the state police and the ABI." Explaining, Jake told Rachel that the ABI was the Alabama Bureau of Investigation. Since no state lines had been crossed, the FBI would not help.

"But he said no police, Jake. You can't call them. They may kill her!"

Hearing a noise at the top of the stairs, everyone turned toward the parlor doors. Stomping her feet as she made her descent, Barbara was muttering under her breath. "What's a person got to do around here to get her beauty sleep? I can't lie down for my afternoon nap if the phone keeps ringing and the door keeps getting banged on!" Stopping at the foot of the stairs and seeing the expressions on everyone's face, Barbara knew immediately that something else had happened. Finally settling on Oscar, Barbara asked him what happened. Sitting quietly on the couch while Oscar and Jake told her everything, Barbara did her best to keep calm. When they were through speaking, she exploded at Jake saying, "Why aren't you out there looking for my daughter? Rachel doesn't need you sitting here holding her hand...I can do that! You'd better hope they haven't harmed one hair on her head, or both of you gentlemen will be answering to me! Now get out and go find her!"

Shocked by Barbara's outburst, Dora went to her side and tried to calm her down. Looking at each other, both Jake and Oscar stood up to leave. Rachel followed them to the door saying, "Don't take her anger personally. You've got to understand, my grandmother is old and has already lost one daughter to this crazy person."

Speaking to Oscar, Jake said, "Go out to your car and wait for me, I'll just be a minute." Turning back to Rachel he said, "She's right, Rachel, we do need to be out looking for your mother. I'll call if I have any news. In the meantime, keep the doors locked and stay inside." Starting to leave he came back and asked, "Are Ollie and the others still working at the chicken house?" Rachel shook her head yes in response to his question. "I'll go speak to them before I leave." Pulling her gently into his arms he kissed her deeply. Sighing as he pulled away from her, Jake said, "Try not to worry, I'm gonna find your mother. I'll bring her home safe and sound. That's a promise." The doubt and tears in Rachel's eyes were killing him. Tilting her head up with his forefinger, Jake smiled and said, "Rachel, I never break a promise. Trust me, okay?"

Doing her best to smile back at him, Rachel replied, "I do trust you Jake. I always have."

"That's my girl," he said and kissed her again. "Now go inside, and lock the door like I said."

"Yes, sir!" Turning, she went back inside and locked the door. Jake stood on the porch until he heard the door latch turn. Taking the front steps in one leap he headed toward Oscar.

* * * * *

Later that evening, Jake and Deputy Wheeler returned carrying some kind of equipment. Rachel had been looking out the window in the study and saw them drive up. Going to the door, she opened it before they could knock. After greeting her with a warm embrace, Jake asked where everyone was. Rachel told him that her grandmother was in the kitchen with Dora. Eyeing the equipment he carried, Rachel asked what it was.

Walking into the parlor and over to the phone he said, "This is a recording device that I am going to connect to your phone. Charlie is going to stay and monitor any calls you get. It may be the only lead we get, and if we can trace the call we can find Sherry that much faster."

Alarmed, Rachel exclaimed, "But Jake, he said no police!"

"Rachel, trust me, he won't know we are tracing the call. Besides, I didn't let Charlie bring his car, and he's dressed in civilian clothes. If anyone sees him they will think he is a relative or something."

Speaking for the first time, Charlie said, "I'm gonna stay out of sight, Ms. Collier. No one but you and Mrs. Parker will know I'm here."

Finally agreeing that the calls did need to be traced, Rachel relented and said the deputy could stay.

* * * * *

Her eyes growing accustomed to the dark room, Sherry took in her surroundings. Very little light was coming through the one window in the room, so she knew it would be night soon. She was in what looked like an old abandoned cabin. The only thing in the room was a small bed, which she was occupying, an old scarred up table and two mismatched chairs. A gag was in her mouth. Her hands were tied behind her back with a rope that was also attached to her feet and neck. If she tried to straighten out her legs, she would choke herself. She didn't know how long she could stay in this position without getting a leg cramp.

Earlier, when her abductor had brought her here, she heard him talking to someone. She couldn't hear either voice very well, because of the blindfold over her head. Keeping her blindfolded, they had put a phone to her ear and told her to speak to Rachel. Thankful Rachel was all right and that someone knew she was missing, Sherry tried to listen to the men's voices. One of them sounded familiar, but she could not place where she had heard it before. The men had left one at a time, with the last one leaving about an hour ago. At least he had taken the blindfold off before he left. Unfortunately, the man had a mask over his face and she could not see who it was. She didn't know how long it would be until one of them returned.

Thinking now may be the only chance she had to try and escape, she looked around the room again. Spotting a small knife on the table, she attempted to get off the bed. The only way off was to roll, but either way she rolled she took a chance of hurting herself. Going limp as she fell to the floor prevented her from getting hurt. Landing on her side, she inched her way sideways across the floor. The length of the rope kept her to a slow crawl, but eventually she made it to the table. Using her shoulder, she nudged the table, testing to see how heavy it was. Finding that it was flimsy because one leg was shorter than the others, she smiled through the gag, said a prayer and pushed harder.

On the third push the table flipped onto its side. The knife skidded across the floor away from her. Again crawling, she wormed her way toward the knife. Turning so her back was to the knife, she managed to get one hand on it and position it against the rope. The knife was dull and it took all her strength to saw it into the rope. Feeling the rope start to unravel renewed Sherry's hope that she could get free.

The first part of the rope that she cut through was to her legs. Stretching them, she could feel them tingle as the blood started to circulate once again. Slowly sitting up and carefully turning the knife around, she then cut the piece that held her neck. With that finally done, she tried to turn the knife around so she could cut the rope off her hands, but she soon realized that she could not get the right angle on the rope to cut it without cutting her wrists. They were already raw from struggling against the rope. Sitting on the floor, she thought of another way. Putting the knife on the floor, she pushed it a small distance away from her. What she was about to try was going to be hard but it was her only chance. Sitting on her hands and rolling her shoulders forward, Sherry painfully slid her rear end through her hands. It took some wiggling and a lot of praying, but one leg at a time she pulled them through her hands. For the first time in her life, Sherry was thankful for having short legs, and when she got home she would have to thank her mother for the gymnastic lessons she had as a child. Picking the knife up again she sawed at the rope on her wrists. Once they were free she untied the gag from her mouth.

Sherry felt her legs stinging like needles were being stuck in them when she attempted to stand. Taking slow and steady steps toward the cabin door, she listened for any noise that would indicate someone's approach. Opening the door just a crack she peeked outside. There was still enough daylight left to see the perimeter of the clearing in front of the cabin. No one was around. Her legs beginning to feel normal again, she thought it was now or never. Sprinting through the clearing, Sherry reached the dirt road that led to the cabin. Thinking it would be safer if she went through the woods in case one of the men returned, she walked parallel to the dirt road.

Finally, after walking about a mile through the woods, Sherry came to a paved highway. The problem was she didn't know where she was or what highway she had reached. Looking at the last of the sunrays that filtered through the pines, she decided the highway ran north to south. Going by instincts, she started walking south.

The road was not very wide and it had not been resurfaced in a long time. There were hardly any shoulders to the road at all. The forests on both sides were so close they cast long and dark shadows over the road. Hearing a car coming behind her, she managed to jump behind a tree without being seen. Since she had no idea who her abductors were or where they had gone, she would have to be careful and not be seen on the highway.

As darkness fell, Sherry continued walking in what she hoped was the right direction. There was no moon tonight and visibility was poor, with patches of fog making it even more difficult to see. She guessed she had seen maybe five or six vehicles pass since she had started walking. Hearing what sounded like a large truck coming, she again left the road and hid. The lights of the truck passed by her, and as they did she caught a glimpse of a road sign. Reading it quickly before the truck lights were gone she read that Evergreen was thirty miles away. Her feet and legs were aching from so much walking and she realized she would not be able to go much further on foot.

Deciding to take a chance on the next car that passed, Sherry walked back up onto the highway. She continued walking as she prayed for a vehicle to come by. After what seemed like an hour, a car finally came around the curve behind her. Stepping to the side of the road, she attempted to flag it down. The car slowed down and came to a stop a few feet further up the road. Taking off at a run toward the car before the person changed their mind, she went to the passenger side and opened the front door of the car. Leaning her head in she said, "Oh! Thank God! It's you!"

"Are you all right?" asked the man.

"Yes, just scared! I've been kidnapped and managed to get away. Take me home please!"

"Of course, where else would I take you?"

Breathing a sigh of relief, she settled into the seat. So thankful that someone she knew had come by, Sherry didn't see the blow coming. She was punched so hard that her head slammed into the door window. Slumping sideways against the door, she was out cold.

Anger boiled through the man. He had been searching for her for over an hour. That idiot he had helping him had screwed up again. He still wasn't sure how she had managed to get untied, but it wouldn't happen again. He would make sure of it this time. Now that she knew who he was, he definitely would make sure she didn't get away. He had plans to get rid of her as well as her daughter soon. Driving back to the cabin, he dragged her from the car and took her inside. She was still unconscious when he chained her wrists to the iron bed railing. Satisfied that she wasn't going anywhere this time, the man left to finish his plans for the night.

CHAPTER TWELVE

Deputy Wheeler did as he said and stayed out of sight. He was so quiet Rachel almost forgot he was there. With every hour that passed waiting for the phone to ring, Rachel became more nervous. She was pacing the parlor floor when Barbara came in and said, "Rachel, honey, you're going to wear a hole in that carpet. Why don't you find something to occupy yourself? Go in the study and work on the books, or something. You can hear the phone ring in there."

Agreeing with Barbara, Charlie said, "I'll come find you Ms. Collier, if the phone rings."

"Okay, but I'll just be in the study," she replied. Walking across the foyer and into the study, Rachel decided to leave the doors open so she wouldn't miss the phone ringing.

Standing at the window looking outside she realized it had gotten dark. There was no moon out tonight, and with the porch light off she couldn't see anything. Moving to the desk on the other side of the room she sat down and looked for something to do. She had the records all up to date, but she booted the computer up anyway. Once it was on, she started exploring some of Darlyn's folders that she had not looked at before now.

Opening the folder marked miscellaneous, Rachel again read through the daily activities that were recorded here. Scrolling through them, she found a sub-folder that she had not seen before. Curious, she opened it. Not understanding it at first, she kept studying it. After a few minutes she realized it was a formula of some kind. There were no notes or worksheets with the formula to help her analyze it further. Getting frustrated with it, she gave up and closed the folder.

Shutting down the computer, she sat there and looked around the room. *Now what can I do*, she thought. Crossing her legs, she bumped her knee on the desk drawer. Pulling the drawer out, she started looking through it. She found only the usual desk supply stuff in this drawer. Reaching into the very back of the drawer and pulling everything forward, she sorted through the pens, paper clips and other odds and ends that had shifted to the back. Along with the odds and ends was a small brass key. Not sure what it went to she put it back in the drawer and closed it. Next she pulled out the bottom drawer on the right side of the desk and started going through the folders. Most of these were hardcopy duplicates of what was in the computer. Reaching the miscellaneous file, she took it out and placed it on top of the desk. Starting at the beginning of the file, she found newspaper clippings and copies of letters to different people.

* * * * *

Now that it was dark enough and she knew Rachel was occupied in the study, Barbara quietly went down the back stairs and out the back door. She had told Deputy Wheeler where she was going so they wouldn't ask any questions. Charlie had promised to let Dora know when he went outside to make his rounds, so Dora could keep an eye on Rachel. Earlier that evening Barbara had pulled her car around to the back of the house, facing the lane. Rachel would not be able to hear the car start if she was in the study. Slowly and without headlights, Barbara started up the lane. Once she reached the highway, she turned the headlights on. Praying for her daughter's safety, Barbara drove toward Evergreen down Highway 31. Several miles before town, she turned off the highway and onto a dirt road. Driving carefully down the long, twisting dirt road she finally came to her destination. By the number of vehicles parked outside the cabin, she knew she was the last to arrive. Getting out of the car and going to the cabin, she didn't knock on the door; instead she just walked on in. Several men and a woman were in the room standing around a table looking at a map of the area.

As Barbara squeezed around the table with the others, Jake said, "Good. Now that everyone is here, we can get started. I don't think the kidnappers have taken Ms. Collier very far. With that in mind, I have marked every abandoned cabin or old trailer I can think of. We'll divide the area into sections and search each of these places. Does everyone have a radio?" Looking around to make sure everyone did, he continued, "Okay, I want you to report anything that looks remotely unusual." Looking up at one of the other men he asked, "Are your people ready to move?"

"Yes, they're in place."

"Good. We'll use this cabin as our base. Everything should be reported back here. Does anyone have any questions?" When no one answered, he looked at Barbara and said, "Ms. Barbara, I know how anxious you are for us to find Ms. Collier. I promise, we'll do everything in our power to find her."

"I know you will," she responded. Going to a chair she sat down while they finished making their plans.

* * * * *

Taking the folder to the couch, Rachel sat down and started reading from the beginning. Things were starting to make sense to her now. The first newspaper clipping was about a local farm going out of business. The woman selling the farm was not available for comment. The second clipping was about an accident on another farm several months later, killing the owner, and the farm being auctioned off. The next object in the folder was a list of ingredients for something. Setting that paper to the side she continued looking through the folder.

So engrossed in what she was doing, Rachel did not hear Charlie as he went out the back door to make his rounds. He had promised the sheriff that he would check on things at the chicken house to make sure nothing was wrong. While he was outside he decided to stop for a smoke as well. Standing at the side of the lane leading to the chicken house he pulled out his lighter. Just before he lit it, he saw two figures creeping toward him. Dropping the lighter, Charlie reached for his gun. One of the figures jumped him before he could aim. Fighting over the gun, he did not see the other figure come at him from behind. Suddenly, he felt a sharp pain in his ribs as a knife was plunged into him. As the deputy fell to the ground, one of the men caught him and dragged him to the underbrush, leaving him there to die. The last thing Charlie remembered seeing was the dark shadows of the men as they started for the house. He never saw the other two figures approach from the trees.

* * * * *

Angry that Rachel had involved the police, the boss and the other man stopped at the back of the house. Looking around the boss said, "I don't think there are any more cops around, but just in case there are, I want you to stay out here and take care of them." Snidely, he asked, "Do you think you can handle that?" Not waiting for an answer the boss walked stealthily to the back door of the house. Finding the back door unlocked he crept inside.

* * * * *

Beginning to understand everything she was reading, Rachel settled back on the couch, stretching out her legs. Her back was to the door so she didn't see the man as he came into the room and silently slid the doors closed. Feeling the presence of someone watching her, Rachel sat up and looked behind her, the contents of the folder falling unnoticed to the floor. Standing before her was a man dressed all in black with a mask over his head, pointing a pistol at her. Her hands flying to her mouth in fright, she started to scream for help, but only a squeak came out. *How did he get in here*, she thought. Where was the deputy? Had he hurt her grandmother and Dora?

Laughing at her, the man said, "Well now, what do we have here?"

Finding her voice Rachel whispered, "Who are you? What do you want?"

"Who I am doesn't matter. What I want does." Stepping closer to Rachel, he again laughed as she stepped backward, away from him. Never taking his eyes off of her, the man bent down and retrieved the folder and papers from the floor.

"Well, this is just what I was looking for. Thanks for saving me the trouble of looking for it. Your aunt was a big pain in my side; she thought she was so smart. But I took care of her, just like I'm going to take care of you." Before she could stop him, he grabbed her by the arm and took her to the desk. Pushing her roughly into the chair, he pulled a packet of papers from under his shirt and placed them on the desk. Unfolding the papers he handed her a pen and said, "Now sign this."

"What is it?" she asked, stalling for time.

Waving the gun in front of her face he said, "You're so smart, I think you can figure out what it is."

Reluctantly she took the pen from him, and skimmed the paper with her eyes. The paper he wanted her to sign was a bill of sale for the farm.

Forgetting her fear and letting the anger that was built up inside of her take over, she threw the pen at his face, screaming, "I won't sign this paper, and you can't make me!"

Snarling at her the man said, "You're forgetting something aren't you, Ms. Collier? You do want to see your mother again, don't you?"

Horror and fear for her mother's life made Rachel rethink the situation. There was still no sign of the deputy, her grandmother or Dora. "You wouldn't harm her, would you?"

Knowing he had her where he wanted her, he leaned over her and answered, "I will if you don't sign these papers."

A plan forming in her mind, Rachel said, "I won't sign this until I see for myself that my mother is all right. Take me to her, and then I'll sign them." If she could get to Sherry, maybe the two of them could escape together. If not, then at least she would know that her grandmother was safe with the man out of the house. The man's cold, calculating eyes looking at her from behind the mask made Rachel shiver in fear. She could tell he was thinking about what she had said.

"Okay, if that's what you want." Taking her by the arm, again he manhandled her. Dragging her out from behind the desk and pushing her toward the doors, he said, "Don't try anything stupid or you won't see your mother or anyone else. Do you understand?" Feeling the pistol in her back, she nodded her head yes and started for the door.

Just before Rachel opened the door, they heard a gunshot outside. Her eyes wide with fear, she looked back at the man. Anger flashed from his eyes as he said, "Well, looks like we have company. Come on!" Sliding only one of the doors open, Rachel stepped out of the room and into the darkened foyer. Hesitating for only a moment, she felt the gun in her back forcing her to go on.

*   *   *   *   *

Deputy Wheeler had never come back from his rounds and Dora was worried that something had happened to him. Standing outside the study doors, Dora had heard everything that was said between Rachel and the intruder. She had to do something to help her. Quietly, Dora went into the parlor and took a log from the stack of firewood by the fireplace. Taking the log into the foyer she hid beside the study doors and waited. Timing was critical to what Dora had planned. As Rachel stepped into the foyer, Dora stuck out her foot and tripped her.

Stumbling, Rachel fell on the floor, never seeing what caused her to trip. The swish of something flying through the air over her head made her look back at the man. With Rachel watching in astonishment, Dora swung the log with all her strength at the man's face. The sound of bones cracking could be heard as the log smashed into him, rendering him unconscious. Falling forward, the man landed on top of Rachel, knocking the breath out of her.

Throwing the log aside, Dora helped Rachel out from under the man. "Are you all right, Ms. Rachel?" she asked, as they stood up.

Hugging Dora tightly, she said, "Yes, thank you, I'm fine."

Suddenly, the front door crashed open. Standing in the doorway with guns drawn was Jake and several of his deputies. The excitement and stress of everything she had gone through in the last hours pressed down on Rachel, and she felt she couldn't take any more. The vision she thought she saw behind Jake was too much, and she fainted at Dora's feet. Rushing to Rachel's side, Jake picked her up and carried her to the parlor. Leaving her on the couch, he came back to the foyer. Kneeling beside the intruder, he pulled the mask off the man's face. Blood was congealing around his nose and mouth, but they could still recognize him. "Is he dead?" asked the woman standing beside him.

Recognizing the intruder, Jake said to the woman, "No, he's alive. You were right all along."

"He's still not the one I want," she said.

Motioning for his men to take the man into custody, he continued, "Why don't you and Ms. Barbara go check on Rachel, while my men and I clean up this mess."

"Of course. She's going to have a lot of questions when she wakes up." Following Barbara and Dora, she went into the parlor with them. Dora turned on a lamp, while Barbara sat down on the love seat and waited for Rachel to wake up.

Unable to contain her fears any longer, Barbara asked, "Do you think Sherry is still alive?"

Standing above her, the woman tried to reassure her, saying, "I'm sure she is. The police are on their way to get her as we speak. We both heard what the policemen told Jake over the radio. The man they captured outside told them where she is."

"Yes, you're right, I'm just being my usual worrisome self. Thankfully this is almost over with."

Interrupting, Dora asked, "Can I get you anything, Ms. Barbara?"

Taking Dora's hand and squeezing it, Barbara answered, "Yes, you can pour me a brandy. Then, I guess, you'll need to put some coffee on to brew. Looks like we will be up most of the night talking to Rachel and Sherry. We have a lot of explaining to do, don't we, Darlyn?"

"Yes, Mother, we do," she answered, taking a seat next to Barbara.

*　*　*　*　*

Regaining consciousness, Rachel could hear voices around her, and she instinctively opened her eyes and tried to sit up. Looking at Darlyn, she whispered, "You're not dead?"

"No, Rachel, I'm alive and well." Continuing, Darlyn said, "Now I'm sure you have a thousand questions, but if you don't mind, let's wait until your mother gets here. Okay?"

Rachel started to protest; however, Jake walked into the room, followed by a deputy. The deputy was escorting a prisoner. "Darlyn, is this the person who tried to kill you?"

"Yes, that's the man, Jake. Who is he?"

This time Rachel spoke up saying, "What do you mean, who is he? That's Guy Hicks, the gardener you hired."

Astonished, Darlyn looked at Rachel and said, "Rachel, you know I've never had a gardener. Where did you get that idea?"

"From Ollie; he said you hired him."

Jake interrupted the women saying, "Guy, why would Ollie say Mrs. MacKinstry hired you?"

Staring at the floor, Guy answered, "'Cause, the boss told me to tell him that." Raising his eyes to meet Jake's, he added, "I ain't saying nothing else. So don't ask me no more questions."

"That's all I needed to know for now. Sammy, you can take the prisoner away now. I'll be in later to question him further. Oh, Sammy, how is Charlie doing?"

"He's stable sir, and on his way to the hospital as we speak."

No one said anything else until the deputy had left with Guy. Rachel had started to get her senses back, and along with them a strong feeling of anger took over. Exploding in an emotional outburst, she cried, "Someone better start talking! What's going on? Guy wasn't the man in the study. Who was that? Was it the boss that Guy referred to? And what happened to Deputy Wheeler?"

Jake answered Rachel, saying, "He was stabbed while making his rounds. We had others stationed outside who found him and called us. That's how we got here so fast."

Speaking up for the first time, Barbara said, "Rachel, calm down this minute. We will explain everything to you in good time, but not until your mother gets here."

Taking Jake by the arm, Rachel asked, "Is my mother really okay? They didn't hurt her did they?" In answer to her questions, Sherry walked into the room followed by Oscar. The bruise on Sherry's face where she had been punched hours earlier was starting to turn colors and swell, but that was the only sign of injury that Rachel could see. Rushing into Sherry's arms, Rachel hugged her as tight as she could saying, "Mama, are you really all right? God, I was so worried."

Patting Rachel on the back, Sherry said, "Yes, baby, I'm fine, thanks to Oscar and his people."

Standing back and looking at Oscar, Rachel replied, "You mean his workers helped find you?"

"No, honey, I mean his agents."

Totally confused, Rachel sat back down on the couch and said, "I don't care who starts, but somebody better tell me what's been going on."

Sitting next to Rachel on the couch, Sherry added, "Yeah, I'd like to know how my sister raised up from the dead too!"

"I guess I will explain since it all started with me, if that's all right with everyone." Everyone seemed to be in agreement that Darlyn should explain everything to Rachel and Sherry.

"About a year ago, I started having a drop in my egg production. Each month it got a little worse. I started monitoring everything from the temperature in the coops to the amount of water and feed they consumed. Nothing was out of the ordinary. I could find no reason for my hens to stop laying as many eggs as they had in the past. Then other things started to happen. I caught someone breaking into the house one night and I took a shot at him. I thought I had hit him, but I couldn't be sure.

"It was about that time I started reading in the newspaper about other farms in the area. For one reason or another they were going out of business. I tried contacting some of the owners to see if any of them had experienced anything similar to what my farm was going through. The first person I contacted would not respond, so I tried another. The owner of the second farm had been killed in a freak accident, so I tried the third one on my list. The owner called me one night and warned me to be careful, and that she would be sending me something in the mail. It arrived, just as she promised, a few days later. At first I couldn't make heads or tails out of what it was supposed to be. Then a couple of days later it suddenly came to me. What the woman sent me was a list of ingredients in the feed for livestock and poultry. I suspected that Alec was putting something in the feed that was causing the hens egg production to drop. I took a sample of what my hens had been eating and put it aside to send to a friend I have at a laboratory in Birmingham. I thought he might need more than one sample so I started collecting a small bit out of each delivery Alec made."

"Alec Jamison! He was the person behind all this?" asked Rachel.

"That's right. That's who was in the study with you. He was the mastermind behind all this. Anyway, the last time I took a sample, Alec caught me. I'm still not sure what tipped him off, but I was sure he suspected that I was on to him. He came back into the chicken house after I thought he had left. He said he wanted to talk to Ollie about something; never did say what. I didn't want him to see what I was up too, so I got rid of him as quick as I could. Something told me I needed to get what samples I had and send them off that day, and I did just that. I told Ollie I had a doctor's appointment and needed to leave early that day, then I drove straight to town and sent the samples to my friend.

"That night I saw a light at the chicken house. Since I hadn't been there when Ollie locked up for the night, I thought he had left a light on. It was a trap. That man, Guy, was waiting for me. I managed to get out of the chicken house and climb one of the silos. He saw me and followed me up the ladder. I tried to get the door open and push him into the silo, but he overpowered me and started to choke me. When I struggled to get out of his grip, my foot slipped and I fell. The next thing I remember was coming to in the mortuary."

Walking to the bar she poured herself a drink and said, "Jake, you take over from there."

"All right," he said. "We got a call from Ollie about four-thirty that morning, saying that Darlyn was dead. He was so distraught we couldn't understand what happened. My deputies and I got here as soon as we could. When we arrived, Ollie was sitting in his truck in shock. We found Darlyn still on the ground where she fell; no one else was around. I sent my deputies to look after Ollie and called Mr. Lynch, the coroner. After that I went back to cover her up with my jacket. That's when I realized she wasn't dead; she was unconscious. Some of her ribs were broken, along with her arm. We found out later that a rib had punctured one of her lungs causing her breathing to be so shallow Ollie thought she was dead. I sent Ollie back to town and waited for Mr. Lynch. Darlyn started coming to just as he got here. She tried to fight us at first, then when she realized who we were, she told us what happened. She needed a doctor's care and I needed to keep her safe. That's when Mr. Lynch and I came up with the plan to hide her away and let everyone think she was dead. That way I could carry out my investigation without anyone knowing what we suspected. Mr. Lynch got Doc Lowery to come to the mortuary and together they reset her arm. Her lung was another matter.

Doc Lowery admitted her to the retirement home in town and was able to look after her. When she had recovered enough we needed another place to hide her, so she's been staying at my Uncle Russell's cabin ever since." Looking at Rachel, he added, "He's the one that took Darlyn to the hospital when you got hurt. You weren't hallucinating that night."

Darlyn broke into the conversation saying, "Russell also brought me to the house that second night you were here. You almost caught me when you came down to the study. I was running the Berkley Program and didn't know the volume was turned up loud enough to be heard upstairs. I barely made it outside before you came down."

Snapping at them, with fire flashing in her eyes, Rachel said, "I'm glad you all got a kick out of making me think I was losing my mind! I think it was inexcusable for you to cause all of us so much worry and grief, telling us Aunt Darlyn was dead!" Turning her anger toward Jake she continued, "How could you be so heartless? Didn't you think of what you were putting my grandmother and mother through?"

Jake snapped right back at her, "Yes, I did! That's why I called your grandmother that very night. She agreed to keep Darlyn's secret!"

Gasping in shock at Barbara, Rachel asked, "Is that true? Grandmother, did you know all along that Darlyn was alive?"

Defiantly looking at Rachel, Barbara answered, "Yes. I thought it was the best thing to do at the time. And I still do."

Sherry spoke up before Rachel could get into an argument with Barbara, saying, "I still don't understand how Oscar became involved."

"Well, then, let me explain from here," he replied. "Rachel, first you have to know that I'm a retired ABI agent. My former superior with the agency called and said he was sending a couple of agents into my hometown to investigate a report of land fraud. When Ms. Darlyn was reported dead, I went to Jake and told him about our case. I asked to see the coroner's report and he had to tell me what really happened. We suspected that your farm was the next one on the list to be bought out by a dummy corporation, so we worked out a plan that would solve both cases. That's why I insisted on sending some of my workers over to help you out."

Shaking her head in disbelief, Rachel asked, "You mean Maria and Juan are ABI agents?"

"That's right…two of the best I've ever seen."

"Go ahead, Oscar, tell us the rest of it," said Sherry.

"After Maria and Juan got settled in here, they had a chance to snoop around. Yesterday, Rachel, when you went for a walk in the woods, Juan was right behind you. You never saw him did you?" Seeing Rachel shake her head, no, he continued. "They have been keeping an eye on the farm night and day. They were the ones who found Deputy Wheeler and called us. Anyway, we never expected your mother to get kidnapped; that was my screw up. I was late for our date. Sherry, I promise I'll never be late for anything again."

A knock at the parlor doors made everyone turn in that direction. Dora walked in pushing a cart. "You people still hashing this mess out?"

"No, Dora, we're just finishing," said Barbara.

"Well, then, I guess ya'll are ready for some coffee and cake."

Laughing, everyone agreed that they were indeed ready for some. Holding her cup in the air Darlyn said, "To Dora, the woman of the hour. Without you, Alec might have gotten way with his plans tonight."

Showing the biggest smile Rachel had ever seen on her face, Dora said, "Like you always say, Ms. Darlyn, Hens Rule! I wasn't about to let that ol' rooster get away with nothing!"

Her emotions still churning, Rachel slipped from the room. She needed some fresh air and to calm down before she could celebrate. She was thankful that Darlyn was not really dead, but her pride was hurt thinking that her family would keep something this important from her. Leaning against the railing on the front porch, she wondered if her grandmother would ever think of her as an adult and treat her like one. She heard the front door close but did not turn to see who had followed her outside. A warm hand touched her back and she knew immediately that it was Jake. The heat radiating from his body caused her body to respond to his touch.

Jake had been unsure of how Rachel would respond to his caress after the way she yelled at him a short time ago. But he knew he had to make things right between them. He had done some heavy thinking the last two days and realized that he loved Rachel. At first he'd tried to deny it, but the more time he spent away from her the more he knew he had to have her in his life. Sighing softly, he whispered in her ear, "Rachel, I'm sorry. I know you're mad and you have every right to be. I would be if the situation were reversed. Please don't hate me."

Slowly turning into his arms, Rachel said, "Oh, Jake I could never hate you. Don't you know? I love you! That's why it hurt so bad that you didn't confide in me."

Jake's pulse raced when he heard her say she loved him. Pulling Rachel into his arms Jake said, "I love you too." With an emotional kiss they both released all the fears and doubt they had for one another and let their love and respect shine through.

Rachel was the first to pull away. A smile radiating from her face, she looked at him and said, "Come on, let's get out of here."

Laughing he said, "Where do you have in mind going?'

"How about that war zone you call a house."

"All right, but tell me something first."

"I told you I love you. What else do you need to know?"

"What was all that 'Hens Rule' business about?"

This time it was Rachel's turn to laugh. Smiling coyly at Jake, she said, "Oh, I think you'll figure it out eventually."

Epilogue

Things happened fast for the next few months. Deputy Wheeler recovered from his wound, but decided he had been a deputy long enough and retired.

Maria and Ollie started dating on a regular basis. She left the ABI and joined Jake at the sheriff's department, replacing Charlie.

Thanks to the good job by both the sheriff's office and the ABI, the county D. A. was able to make a strong case against Alec and Guy. Alec had planned on acquiring these farms and gaining a monopoly on the state's poultry business. Charged with several counts of land fraud and attempted murder, they would be put away for many years.

At breakfast a couple of mornings after Alec's arrest, Rachel asked Barbara when she was going back to Mobile. Barbara skirted the question until Dora forced her to tell Rachel everything. It turned out the reason Dora and Sherry were trying so hard to get Barbara to stop smoking was because the night that Darlyn was attacked, Barbara had set her house on fire. Barbara had a bad habit of waking up in the middle of the night and, unable to sleep, would lie in bed and read. That particular night she fell back to sleep with a cigarette in her hand. Her book caught fire and fell on the floor. When she woke up the room was full of smoke and fire. Dora managed to get her out in time, thanks to the smoke detector going off, but there was damage to the house, which was being repaired while they were at the farm.

Two days later, Sherry and Oscar announced that they had gone to the courthouse and were married. Now that Rachel knew more about Oscar and who he really was, she was not having those apprehensive feelings toward him any longer. She was happy that her mother had found someone to love, and relieved to know that he would take care of Sherry.

Darlyn had taken over the running of the farm, leaving Rachel without a job. To her satisfaction, she had been hired at the elementary school in Evergreen and would be teaching kindergarten in the fall.

Now, two months after Sherry and Oscar's wedding, Rachel was standing in the vestibule of the church talking to Darlyn. Roxanne had gone inside a few minutes ago. Speaking to Darlyn, Rachel said, "Is Roxanne going to stay mad at you forever?"

"Hardly; we have been friends too long for her to stay mad at me. She'll get used to having me around again. Just this morning at the beauty shop, she was gossiping like old times, telling me all about Bonnie's new beau. It looks like she will be adding that fourth bee to her bonnet real soon." Pointing in the direction of the door, Darlyn added, "See what I mean?"

Turning around in time to see Bonnie enter the church on the arm of a man, she asked, "Well, who is he?"

"That's Bennie Brookes, the banker over at Merchants Bank. Just think, if she marries him they will be Bennie and Bonnie Brookes. Sounds like I'm stuttering, doesn't it!" Giggling like two schoolgirls, Darlyn took Rachel's hand and said, "Are you ready?"

Wearing a Christi original, she said happily, "I've never been more ready for anything in my life."

Rachel walked over to Oscar, placed her hand in his, and together they walked down the aisle. Reaching their places, Oscar smiled at Rachel as he placed her hand in Jake's.

Susan Weekley

About the Author

"When my daughter accused me of spending all the grocery money on books, I decided to entertain myself and started writing."

Ms. Weekley is a former kindergarten teacher and childcare director. For the last twenty years she has worked in the customer service field for two nationwide companies.

Ms. Weekley lives in Semmes, Alabama, and is the mother of two and grandmother of three, (counting the grand-dog). She is currently working on two more books. Watch for the third installment of the Evergreen saga, *Meddling Maggie*!